Dance, Kayla!

Dance, Kayla!

DARWIN MCBETH WALTON

ALBERT WHITMAN & COMPANY
MORTON GROVE, ILLINOIS

Library of Congress Cataloging-in-Publication Data

Walton, Darwin McBeth.
Dance, Kayla! / by Darwin McBeth Walton.
p. cm.
Summary: Brown-skinned, green-eyed Kayla uses her dancing to help deal with her plight when her grandmother's death and the continued absence of her dancer father cause her to leave her farm and live in Chicago with relatives.
ISBN 0-8075-1453-5
[1. Fathers and daughters–Fiction. 2. Farm life–Fiction. 3. Dance–Fiction. 4. Chicago (Ill.)–Fiction. 5. Afro-Americans–Fiction.] I. Title.
PZ7.W1735Dan 1998
[Fic]–dc21
97-27857
CIP
AC

Published in 1998 by Albert Whitman & Company,
6340 Oakton Street, Morton Grove, Illinois 60053-2723.
Published simultaneously in Canada by General Publishing, Limited, Toronto.

Published in the United States of America.
10 9 8 7 6 5 4 3 2 1

The design is by Scott Piehl.

Best wishes

Lainie M. Walton

Contents

Prologue

Kayla looked up from her food into the piercing green eyes of a tall, dark man entering the dining car. She held her breath. Could it be that her daddy had come after all?

It had been a long time—she was four when he last visited. The man stared at her for several seconds and then looked at Aunt Martha. When Aunt Martha flipped the page of her magazine, he hurried on through the car. Kayla's heart sank. Maybe he wouldn't know his daughter, but surely her daddy would have recognized Aunt Martha. She wouldn't have changed much.

Kayla touched the gold locket hanging around

her neck. The train wheels hummed rhythmically and she thought, over and over, "Gran's gone, now what will I do?" With the back of her hand, Kayla wiped her burning eyes. She tried to focus on the dinner plate Aunt Martha had ordered. Much as she loved potato chips, these were hard to swallow. The ham in the sandwich was wet and salty and tasteless, nothing like Granpa's smoked ham.

She thought about Granpa and how he had cried at the funeral.

Kayla hadn't cried then. The tears wouldn't come, even though she had stood between Aunt Martha and Granpa thinking that any minute she herself would surely die. People whispered behind their hands, "Such a tragic thing for Kayla. What a brave girl." Someone said, "Poor thing, what's to become of her?"

Aunt Martha looked at Kayla's practically untouched meal and closed her magazine. She said, "C'mon, honey, let's go. We'll get a bite later." She left money for the bill, and they went back to the coach car where they would ride all night.

To Kayla, the last week was still like a dark and terrible dream. Her life had been changed forever because of the storm. She knew it had brought on Gran's heart attack.

She wanted now—more than ever—to be with her daddy. Where was he? He hadn't come to the funeral. No one had even heard from him.

She clutched her old rag doll for comfort and slumped against the uncomfortable train seat. Over and over she had dreamed about that oddly mixed-up day and dreadful night. Now the rhythm of the train lulled her to sleep, and the dream started again.

CHAPTER ONE

Down on the Farm

Just a week ago, Kayla had awakened with a feeling that something unusual was going to happen. She lay still, watching the white lace curtains fluttering in the wind. "Maybe I'll get the letter from Daddy today...nope, that couldn't be it. Must be something else. Still, it won't hurt to hope for a letter."

She jumped out of bed. From her window she could see bright green cotton bushes glistening in the sun. Way back in the hills, tall pine trees swayed gently in the morning breeze. The scent of magnolia, mixed with Gran's fried bacon, drifted into her room. Except for the spooky feeling, it was like any other summer morning.

She put on her underwear, including a new training bra. Gran said she didn't need it, but wearing a bra made Kayla feel all grown-up. Plus, she would be in sixth grade in the fall.

She slipped a worn sea-green tee-shirt over her head. Her aunt Martha had sent it from Chicago with a note saying it matched Kayla's eyes. Kayla hated people to mention her eyes. She didn't know a single person with green eyes—except her dad. Once, when she was around seven, a kid in the supermarket had yelled to his mom to look at the brown girl with the cat eyes! Everybody had turned to look. The woman had apologized. "Not cat eyes, Jimmy, she has lovely green eyes." Kayla realized then that her eyes were unusual for a brown-skinned person.

She picked up a heart-shaped locket from the table and ran her fingers over the design around the edge. A tiny pearl glowed from the center. She opened the locket and gazed lovingly at miniature photos of her mother and daddy. Then she hooked the delicate link chain around her neck. She put the locket on every morning, and it was the last thing she took off at night. Daddy had sent it for her sixth birthday.

"Hey, Kayla!" A familiar voice came from outside.

"Wanna go fishin'?"

Kayla went to the window. Cheefus, the boy who lived on the neighboring farm, was standing near the magnolia tree. She rested her arms on the sill. "Why you askin' *me*? Did everybody die or run away from home or somethin'?"

"Nobody can go," he grumbled. "Jamie and Diggy had to go to the dentist." He moved his bare foot around in the sand. "Ma has a hankerin' for some catfish. You remember that big one I caught in March? I been tryin' to catch the mate. Ma's been braggin' about me being such a good fisherman and all, so I thought I'd try and catch it for her Mother's Day present."

Kayla said, "Mother's Day is past."

"I know, but I didn't get her nothin'."

"A catfish ain't much better than nothin'."

"Well, that's what she wants. But she won't let me go by myself. She said too many weird things happenin' these days, even way out here on the farm. She keeps remindin' me of that kid's body they found down by the river three years ago."

"So you want me to bodyguard you."

"Ah, Kay, you know I ain't scared, but two is

better'n one." His brown eyes pleaded with her.

Kayla looked at him and smiled. Here he was begging her to go instead of her wishing he would ask. "Have to do my chores first. I'll phone if I can't go."

She turned from the window, picked up her rag doll, Angel, and plopped her in the middle of the white pine dresser. "Boys! They sure hate to need us girls. Almost never can tell about how they feel."

She pulled the pink chenille bedspread over the pillows, then sat at the dresser and unbraided her long black hair, brushed it, put on a dab of hair dressing, and rebraided it into two thick braids. "How you think I'd look in skinny braids with beads?" she asked Angel. "I'm gonna get some when Daddy comes. Then I'll look like Stephanie."

An autographed picture of ballerina Stephanie Dabney gazed at her from a lucite frame. Ms. Pickens, her gym teacher, had brought it from New York last summer, along with a poster of the Harlem Dance Troupe. Kayla studied the dance attitude Stephanie struck in the photo, then picked up a worn blue book from the bedside table and opened it. With her hand on the back of the chair for balance, she began to do warm-up exercises. Bending her long legs, she went slowly up and down, saying aloud, "Straight back, tuck behind. Up on half-toe and down, one, two, three, four, up..."

Every morning she looked at the book and practiced. Every day she danced in the wide hallway that ran down the middle of the farmhouse. She would put a record on Gran's old record player and rehearse the steps Ms. Pickens had taught her for the school play last winter. When she finished her routine, she said to Angel, "I'll dance for Daddy when he comes. Maybe someday he'll let me dance with him, just like Mama did."

Kayla practiced carefully, paying close attention to the pictures in her book. But she knew it wasn't good enough. More than anything in the world, she wanted to take real dancing lessons.

Gran called from the kitchen, "Kaay-la, breakfast is ready. You up, girl?"

"Comin', Gran!" Kayla pulled on her jeans. She threw a kiss at Angel and pirouetted down the hallway. She waltzed into the kitchen. Balloo, the family dog, came out from under the table and wagged his tail furiously until Kayla stopped dancing, curtsied, and patted him on top of his red head.

Gran applauded briefly. She was standing at the old-style gas stove on the west side of the big open room. Pots and pans hung from the ceiling on old-fashioned iron hooks. From the corner windows Gran's vegetable garden could be seen, and a huge fig tree loaded with shiny green figs blocked the view of the chicken yard.

Granpa was finishing his first course, cornflakes and bananas, and thumbing through the *Farmer's Almanac.*

"Mornin', Granpa." Kayla hugged him and brushed her cheek against his big scratchy mustache.

Granpa pointed to the book. "Says here we in for some rainy weather this summer. Hope it doesn't drown out the cotton. We'll be in pretty good shape if this crop makes it."

Kayla ignored the cornflakes and piled scrambled eggs, grits, bacon, and a fluffy biscuit on her plate. She picked up her fork.

"Say the blessing," ordered Gran.

Kayla knew Granpa had said his blessing, but

he bowed his head again. Kayla put her fork down and said, "Thank you, God, for the food we're about to receive for the nourishment and strength of our bodies. Amen."

"Amen," repeated Gran and Granpa.

Granpa put ham, eggs, and a biscuit on his plate. Looking at Kayla's plate, he said, "Well now, honey girl, if you manage to wrap yourself around all that food, I might let you cut a few logs and kill a few hogs for the church barbecue."

Kayla screwed up her face and stuffed a large piece of biscuit topped with peach preserves into her mouth. She hated hog-killing time. She didn't even like killing chickens, but she was old enough to know it had to be done.

They ate silently for several minutes. Kayla said at last, "Hey, Granpa, you remember the time when our sow had thirteen baby pigs and we had to nurse 'em with baby bottles?"

"Sure do. Thirteen was a record 'round here, and we didn't lose a one." Granpa pushed his chair back and stood up slowly, holding on to the big table. "My ole bones tell me it's gonna rain today, and this rememberin' won't get my chores done. Walt and

I are goin' to Columbia for supplies first thing." He stood holding the screen open. "You been doin' a mighty fine job taking care of Ancy, honey girl— she looks good. In a day or so she'll be ready to calve. Check on her two, three times. Your granma knows what to do if she gets fretful. Any trouble, call Zack."

"Sure, Granpa." Kayla lowered her voice. "Cheefus asked me to go fishin', if it's okay."

Nobody said a word. Finally Gran smiled and said, "Oh, he did, did he?"

Kayla felt her cheeks get warm. "Everybody's busy and Aunt Minnie won't let him go by himself." She giggled. "I'm going to protect him, if you can spare me." She looked at Gran.

"Sure, honey girl. Fish for lunch sounds good."

Kayla helped Gran clear the table. "What time you leavin', Granpa?"

He took a toothpick out of his shirt pocket and stuck it in his mouth. "Soon's I look after Ancy. I'll eat my fish for supper."

Wilesy, their calico cat, dashed up the steps and slipped in through the open door. Kayla picked her up. "Aha, you smelled the bacon, I bet. Huntin' not too good, huh, girl?"

"Huntin' indeed," said Gran. "Bet she hasn't caught a mouse all year. Every time I open the fridge, she's curlin' round my legs, mewin'."

"She likes milk with her meat, huh, kitty?" said Kayla. "Remember, we don't have mice in the house or even in the cellar."

"Now, that's true and it's beyond me, 'cause the bloomin' cat never goes to the cellar unless we go first. I think she's afraid of the dark."

"Maybe there's a ghost down there," suggested Kayla. She put the cat down and scraped the left-overs into her dish. She put the dishes in the dish-pan and ran hot water on them. "I heard dogs and cats can see ghosts even when people can't."

"Well, there're no ghosts down there. We'd have heard them ourselves after all these years. Don't for-get, I was born in this house, and so was your mom."

"Yes'm, I know, and she died in it, too," said Kayla. She realized that the talk was turning serious. She warmed up Gran's coffee before sitting down next to her. "Gran, I never told you, but I believe Mama's ghost comes on my birthday. Every year. I always thought I was dreaming until this year. I was wide awake when she came and stood at the foot of my bed and said, 'Happy birthday, baby.' "

Gran put a little sugar in her coffee. "Now, honey girl, you were dreaming. I never much believed in ghosts myself."

"I know, Gran, me neither. But she sure looked real. Her dress was white, and there was a blue light all around her. Course it could have been my guardian angel. I have one for sure. *Somebody* stopped me from steppin' on that old rattler last year." Kayla got up and went to the sink to begin washing dishes. After a moment she asked, "But who else died in this house?"

"The other ones I know of were my granpa and granma."

"Tell me again about how they died," said Kayla.

Gran finished her coffee and got up from the table. "Here, I'll wash, honey girl; you dry." She picked up a plate. "Well, now, you know that my granpa, Hezekiah, was a slave—just a boy when the Civil War broke out. He and his mother, Adefy, stayed on at the Big House until long after the war was over. The plantation owner, who was Hezekiah's father, gave this house and land to Adefy when his wife died.

"Later on Granpa Hezekiah married Rena, a Cherokee Indian girl. Her hair was so long she could sit on it. I remember brushing it on summer nights while we sat on the porch. It would sparkle like stars. We were sitting right here in front of the fire one winter night, popping corn, when she just up and died. Real peaceful. Without even a deep breath." Gran looked at Kayla and continued. "Granpa Hezekiah died a year later of a broken heart, because he didn't like living without Granma Rena. That's the way I want to go, peaceful like Granma Rena did."

Gran wiped her hands on the kitchen towel and said, "Good gracious, all this talk about death! Go on, honey girl, feed the dog and chickens. I'll finish up here."

Kayla took Balloo's yellow dish to the pantry and poured in two cups of dog food from a bag. She added a few table scraps. Balloo knew what was happening. When Gran said, "Feed the dog," he had come out from under the table and followed Kayla around until she set the dish on the hearth. She filled his water dish, too, before going to the chicken yard.

Outside, Kayla scooped chicken feed from a large plastic barrel and scattered it on the ground.

For a while she watched the chickens scramble over one another to get food.

Then Kayla ran to the barnyard. Ancy was standing under a tree, chewing contentedly. Granpa was in the barn putting fresh hay in Ancy's stall. "She looks okay to me," yelled Kayla.

Granpa came to the barn door. "Yep, she looks pretty good. A mite unsettled, but that's regular, being it's her first calf."

Kayla took the old metal pail that was slung over a fence post and went to get water from the yard pump. When she came back, she picked up a frayed towel from a basket, wet it, and washed Ancy's face. She went into the barn. "You take her temper'ture, Granpa?"

"I did already. It's up a smidgeon, not enough to count."

Kayla plopped down in the hay and stuck the end of her braid in her mouth. "I can't wait to see the calf. Remember, you told me Ancy's first calf would be mine if I took care of Ancy. Can I watch it being born, Granpa?"

Granpa took off his cap, and scratched his thick grey hair. "Don't see why not. It's your calf."

"Thanks, Granpa. If I don't get to be a dancer, I may be a veter'narian when I grow up. Will you wake me up if it comes in the middle of the night?"

"Don't see why not," he said again. "Sometimes it's four, five hours after the water breaks b'fore the calving. Don't worry, you'll prob'ly hear Ancy bawlin' when it starts."

"What d'you have to do?" she asked.

"Maybe nothin'. The calf seems in the right position. I might have to give its feet a tug if it's too long a-comin'."

Kayla stood up. "I better get goin'. Cheefus plans to catch the biggest catfish in the river." Without waiting for an answer, she ran out into the morning sun. Balloo met her, wagging his tail. "Hey, fellah, wanna go fishin'?"

Granpa came to the barn door. "Keep an eye on those clouds way over west, and watch where you walk," he called. "Snakes are out and around."

CHAPTER TWO

A Fish Story

Kayla ran across the yard to the path. Cheefus was waiting at the gate, holding a baby garter snake. He handed it to her.

"Oh, he's so cute!" Kayla felt it squirm in her hand for a minute, then set it on the ground. Balloo sniffed and watched it wriggle away. "You dug the worms already?" she asked.

"Sure did. I got a can full." He pointed to the five-gallon pail he was carrying.

"That's a lot of worms," teased Kayla. "You fixin' to catch all the fish in the whole creek?"

Cheefus lifted a coffee can out of the big pail and said impatiently, "Just this here can is full."

"Aw, I know, silly. Just teasin' you."

"Why do girls have to tease 'bout serious things?" he grumbled.

" 'Cause they don't think some things are serious," said Kayla as they started down the path. "Gran says girls think different from boys."

"If you was one o' them worms about to be gobbled up by a fish, you'd think it was serious."

"I wasn't teasin' about the—uh—predicament of the worms," argued Kayla. "I was teasin' about you diggin' five gallons of 'em." She looked down at his bare feet. "Now I notice that you're barefoot. Don't you take rattlesnakes serious?"

"Rattlesnakes run when they hear me comin'," he boasted.

Kayla giggled. Cheefus followed her across the cotton field into the pine forest. About a half-mile into the woods they jumped over a clear, rocky stream which divided Granpa's land from the next farm. On hot days, all the kids went wading in the stream, but today Kayla and Cheefus didn't stop.

"C'mon, I know a place to catch some big ones," Cheefus said. "A spot where nobody goes." He started off at a trot. Kayla and Balloo ran along behind.

The path, lined with daisies and wild strawberries, was paved with pine needles that scrunched softly beneath their feet. An occasional gardenia bush flashed white beyond tangled honeysuckle and blackberry vines. Kayla slowed to a walk. She breathed in the woodsy smells and listened to the songs of birds and rustling of small animals.

"It's just around the bend," said Cheefus, increasing his speed. "Hurry up!"

"Go ahead!" yelled Kayla. "We're coming."

Cheefus reached the creek. He dipped up a bucket of the cold water and settled down to bait his hook.

He had barely put his pole in the water, when a seven-inch bass grabbed the night crawler wiggling on the end of the line. Cheefus let out a yell that echoed through the forest. "Hey, look, Kayla, I got a bass!" He yanked it out of the creek, removed the hook, and threw the wiggling fish into the bucket. By the time Kayla sat down on the creek bank, Cheefus had two fish big enough to keep and was grinning from ear to ear. "What'd I tell ya? Is this a great place or what?"

Suddenly, an uneasy feeling crept up her back.

It was like the feeling she had had earlier in the morning. She looked around, fully expecting to see somebody peeking from behind a tree. Nothing.

Carefully she picked a worm out of the can. "Shoot, I hate it when they wiggle so much."

Cheefus laughed. "The more they wiggle, the faster the fish see them."

"Yeah, I guess." She tossed the line into the creek. "You prob'ly caught all the fish in here anyway." They leaned against a tree and settled down to wait.

School had been out for a week. Kayla loved the hot days. She loved walking barefoot in the warm sand and wading in the icy creek. Sometimes when she and Cheefus searched the woods, they would find baby animals or discover a fruit tree flowering for the first time. The woods were filled with wonder and mystery. The summers were never long enough.

Cheefus broke the silence. "Hear anything from your pa?"

"No. Nothin'. Not since he wrote that he fell off the stage in February and hurt his hip."

"Yeah, I remember. Did he say it was broke?"

"No, just hurt. But that could be bad."

Cheefus looked at her worried face. "Well, you don't die from a broken hip, you know."

"I know, but he might have a hard time dancin' with one." Suddenly her bobber went under, and she felt a pull on her line. "Hey, I got a bite, too!" She yanked at the line the way Granpa had taught her. "Wow, this is some big fish. It's pullin' back!"

"Could be a turtle," said Cheefus. "I'll get the net. Hold steady! Don't let him steal your pole!"

"Hurry Cheefus—he's gonna pull me in!"

Cheefus waded into the thigh-deep creek and swiped at the critter with the net. The net was too small. "You'll have to drag him out!" he yelled. "It's a catfish! Wow, he's a whopper! Must be the mate to mine."

Kayla dug her heels into the mud and pulled the big fish over to the edge of the creek. "Get the line, Cheefus! He'll break it!"

Cheefus grabbed the fishing line about five feet from the hook and crawled up on the bank, dragging the jumping fish with him. "Man, look at that—must be near two feet long!"

Kayla was overwhelmed. "I never saw a fish that big. He must have come in from the river!"

"You mean the *ocean!*" exclaimed Cheefus. "Boy, Mama would be so proud if I'd a-caught that fish." He looked at Kayla. "You wouldn't think of sellin' it?"

"You mean, you'd say *you* caught it?"

"Well, I helped bring him in."

"That's for sure. Tell you what, you can have him and I'll take two of yours. He's too much for us anyway."

"Can I say I caught him?" he asked, lowering his lashes and looking at her sideways .

"You mean you'd lie?" She looked at his face and waited for an answer.

He thought for a few seconds, frowning and screwing up his mouth. "Yeah," he said, jerking his head to agree with himself. "A little lie won't hurt nobody."

Kayla looked at the big ugly fish. "Don't seem worth it to me. C'mon. I hear thunder, and it's gettin' dark. Granpa said it's gonna storm today."

They gathered their things. Cheefus cheerfully carried the fish. The tail of the big one stuck out over the top of the pail.

They hurried back through the woods. When they reached the edge, Kayla said, "I bet your folks'll believe you caught that fish without you tellin' a lie. If they ask, just look surprised and say, 'Who you think caught it, *Kayla?*' Then give a horse laugh and say, 'Oh, sure, Kayla caught it. *Sure* she did!' "

With shining eyes and a big grin, Cheefus looked at Kayla. "Doggonit, Kayla, I wish you was a boy!"

CHAPTER THREE

A Small Miracle

Kayla ate two big pieces of fried fish and helped Gran wash the lunch dishes. Then she picked up a library book and ran to the front porch swing to wait for the mail.

It seemed like she was always waiting for that mail truck. At last, she saw it turn the corner about a half-mile up the road. She jumped off the porch and started up the long driveway.

The sky was getting darker by the minute. The trees were bending with the wind, which glued Kayla's shirt to her thin body. Dirt and sand whipped against her face, stinging her eyes. Balloo started to follow, but halfway down the sandy road he stopped, barked a couple of anxious yaps, then turned around and ran back to the house.

Shielding her face, Kayla peeked through her

fingers and saw Mr. Goodman at the mailboxes. He quickly stuffed them, honked his horn, and waved as he drove off.

She reached their box, crossed her fingers for luck, and pulled out the mail, reading the envelopes one at a time. Nothing from Daddy.

For a moment she forgot the brewing storm. He had promised to visit—"before you're another year older"—he had written in the Christmas note he sent from a theater in Paris, France. Now her birthday had come and gone. Oh, how she wanted to dance and travel all over the world with her daddy! Why didn't he know how much she wanted to hear from him?

Beyond the tall pine trees lightning flashed. It was beautiful and scary at the same time. But Kayla knew she couldn't stay and watch it. Gran was alone waiting for her.

Gran wasn't afraid of much else, but thunderstorms made her nervous. During big storms Gran gathered up her quilt and Bible. Then she and Granpa and Kayla would go down the ladder to the cellar and wait it out. It felt cozy and safe in the cellar, with Gran's canned vegetables and fruits and jams filling the shelves on one wall and Granpa's big sacks of peanuts and potatoes on the other. Kayla remembered thinking, when she was younger, that if they had to stay down there for a spell, it would be a long time before they got real hungry. It was still a comforting thought.

Quickly she pulled the letters from the mailbox next to theirs. Aunt Minnie and Uncle Zack had eight kids including Cheefus, but nobody was in charge of their mail. So Kayla often dropped it off on her way home. She didn't mind. It gave her a chance to see Cheefus. She liked that, especially if he hadn't been around for a while. Uncle Zack and Aunt Minnie were like family. They belonged to the farm co-op that Granpa and Uncle Walt had started over forty years ago. Granpa often told Kayla that the co-op had helped them all hang onto their land and make a decent living.

Kayla saw Cheefus running down the road. "You crazy or somethin'?" he yelled above the wind. "There's a twister warnin' out for these parts. You better get yourself home."

"Where else you think I'm goin'?" she asked, handing over his family's mail.

"Thanks. Did you get anything?" he asked, looking at her with a wide, hopeful grin.

She shook her head, afraid her disappointment would show if she said anything. Tears stung her eyes, and she hoped he wouldn't notice. She knew he had when his face went serious, and he looked down at his bare feet.

Cheefus was twelve, as good-looking as any boy at school. His straight, white teeth fit into his mouth just right. He had big brown eyes with long lashes that made his face come together real nice.

When they reached the fork that divided the path to his house from the path to hers, he said, "Thanks again for the big fish. Mama was so impressed I went ahead and told her you hooked it, but I helped bring 'im in."

"You're welcome," she shouted. "I couldn't a-got it without you."

Halfway down the walk he stopped and turned around. "Want to go to the rope swing after the storm?"

"Okay!" she yelled back.

"Aha," she said to herself. "Two times in one day he asked me to go somewhere. Must have been the fish." She wished Cammie hadn't gone away for the summer. They could have had fun talking about Cheefus asking her to go with him *twice* in one day. That was a record! Kayla ran into the house and dumped the mail on the kitchen table.

Gran was sitting in her upholstered chair, crocheting a shawl. It was red, green, and black—Kwanzaa colors. "I'm almost done," she said. "Just one more row. Your aunt Martha's Christmas *and* Kwanzaa present. Think she'll like it?"

Kayla plopped down in the cane rocker, and Wilesy jumped up into her lap. "It's gorgeous, Gran. She'll love it for sure."

"Any important mail?" asked Gran.

"No ma'am, just two or three catalogs, a couple bills. Nothing important." She examined her dusty, bare feet.

Gran shook her head and sucked her teeth. "Now, honey girl, your dad is galavantin' around the world, prob'ly just making his own ends meet. He'll come when he can. But remember, growin' up is something you have to do for yourself, with or without him." She stopped crocheting and reached out and touched Kayla's knee. "If it has to be without him, well, so be it! You'll do just fine."

Kayla fingered her locket and slipped it back inside her shirt. It felt cool against her bare skin.

A jagged flash of lightning lit the western sky, followed by loud thunder that cracked and rumbled over the house. Gran was crocheting as fast as she could. Anxiously she looked out the window. "Better go check the chicken-yard gate. No tellin' when Granpa and Uncle Walt'll get back. Hurry now. See 'bout Ancy, too. Give her some water. She's not due till day after tomorrow, but you never can tell."

Kayla put Wilesy down. "Let's open the cellar before I go, Gran." She helped Gran move the table closer to the window. A round braided rug covered the opening to the cellar. Kayla folded the rug over to the side, and she and Gran lifted each half of the cellar door. Immediately, Wilesy went down the ladder and found her spot in a dark corner. Kayla laughed at her and ran out the door. "Back in a few minutes, Gran."

The darkening sky had taken on a yellowish color. Alarmed, Kayla jumped off the porch without touching the steps and ran to the chicken house. Except for an occasional cluck or chuckle, the chickens were quiet. The only bird in the yard was the rooster, still strutting around scratching in the dirt. Kayla shooed him into his pen, closed the hatches, and hooked the gate.

Leaves and other flying debris swirled and danced in the yard. The wind grew stronger as she fought her way to the barn. It was dark inside. Kayla pulled the light string as she went in.

Ancy was lying in her stall. Her huge reddish-brown eyes were glassy. She made a long, low sound. "What's the matter Ancy, are you hurtin' real bad?" Kayla rubbed the cow's head gently.

Ancy moaned again and started to breathe great heaving breaths. Kayla noticed that the straw under Ancy was wet. Her water had broken! "Oh for goodness sake!" Kayla cried. "Don't have that calf yet, Ancy! Wait for Granpa. Gran ain't comin' out in this storm." Kayla crouched down and stroked the cow's neck. "It's okay, girl. It'll be okay."

Ancy shivered and groaned loudly. Kayla decided to go for Gran. Then she saw two tiny feet showing beneath Ancy's tail. Too late. "Oh, Lordy, help me," she cried. She knelt down and rubbed the cow's belly. "This is it, Ancy. It's you and me, girl."

Ancy raised her head a bit and lay back with another, more urgent, groan. Now the legs of the calf were showing. Kayla watched for a few minutes, waiting for the head, but nothing else happened.

"Push, Ancy," begged Kayla. She remembered Granpa saying he might have to help. She wished she had asked more questions and paid closer attention. Taking a towel, she grabbed the legs of the calf and pulled—gently at first, then using all her strength. Ancy grunted, and suddenly, the rest of the calf slid out.

Kayla laid the squirming little critter down gently. It was covered with a thin membranelike sac. Ancy stood up and began to lick the calf furiously until the covering was gone. Then she nudged it with her nose, urging it to stand up. After two or three tries, the calf stood on wobbly legs. It somehow managed to find its mother's udder and began sucking as if it had practiced all day.

"We did it, Ancy! We did it, did it, did it! Granpa will get the surprise of his life!" She ran out into the storm.

CHAPTER FOUR

The Storm

Lightning skittered across dark gray clouds, and thunder followed in ear-shattering booms. Between thunderclaps Kayla heard Gran calling, "Kaay-la, come on, hurry in! You hear me?"

Kayla fought her way back across the yard, pushing against the wind and rain. The noise was fearful. In the distance, she saw car lights. She hoped it was Granpa and Uncle Walt. When she reached the house, Balloo crawled from under the back porch and followed her up the steps. Gran opened the door. It took both of them to push it closed again.

"Thank goodness you got in before the storm touched down. Hurry, get down the steps!" Gran commanded.

Kayla caught Balloo's collar and gently pulled him down the ladder.

The flickering light of a kerosene lamp cast eerie shadows on the bushel baskets and burlap bags. There were two beanbags and two folding chairs Gran had bought especially for the cellar. A large round rag rug nearly covered the old wooden floor. Kayla plopped down on one of the beanbags. She was about to tell Gran about the calf when she saw Gran's face grimace with pain. Kayla jumped up and helped Gran unfold one of the chairs. "You okay, Gran?"

"A little indigestion—maybe that fried fish we had for lunch." She frowned again. "I'm real worried about Granpa and Uncle Walt. They must have had to stop on the way home. The storm hit real close by somewhere. That was a big humming under the wind."

"I heard it, Gran, just as I came in." Wilesy came and snuggled up to Kayla, sniffing her face.

"It worried me when you didn't come in right away. What took you so long?"

Kayla laughed happily. "Ancy had the calf, Gran. I helped her, and it's sure a pretty one. *That's* what took me so long! Ancy was ready when I got there. It was wonderful!"

Gran sat up straight, her mouth open, her brown eyes wide. "What did you do?"

"Not much, Gran, just pulled its feet a little."

"Well, glory be. Honey girl, you a constant amazement to me. A veter'narian before you're twelve."

They sat quietly for a while. Kayla touched her locket and whispered, "I bet Daddy would be proud if he knew. I wonder if his agent has been forwardin' my letters. I'll write him again...no, maybe I'll just tell him when he comes."

Gran patted Kayla's shoulder. "He ain't been to see you in eight years!" She rubbed her chest and closed her eyes for a few seconds, then continued quietly. "He came only two times since your mama died, and I wouldn't know him myself if he walked in this minute."

Kayla thought about the old snapshots she had of him and her mother in their costumes. In the latest one, he wore a short beard, and she could barely make out what he looked like. But she could see his eyes—those piercing green eyes. She wondered if she would recognize him now. "He sent my locket, and my ballet book, and my dancing shoes," she said, remembering she had outgrown the shoes three years ago.

"Well, books and shoes are fine, Kayla," continued Gran, "and I know you love that locket to death. But they don't hug you and kiss you and they don't calm no growlin' belly." Gran's voice softened when she looked at Kayla. "Your daddy bein' a dancer in show business and all, no tellin' when he'll be comin'. He sends money once in a while, but he never could promise much. And to be honest, we never expected much."

Kayla didn't want to hear about her daddy not coming. She changed the subject. "I love it down here, Gran. It reminds me of a pirate story I read one time. I think the hold in a pirate ship must look like this, except they have jewels and money instead of jars of jelly and sacks of peanuts."

They heard the kitchen door open and close. Granpa called, "Y'all all right down there?"

"Just fine, Granpa," answered Kayla.

"Well, thank the Lord, he's safe," whispered Gran. She took a deep breath and let it out in a painful sigh.

"The storm's 'bout over. Luckily the twister didn't touch down nearby." Granpa came halfway down the ladder. "'Cept it's rainin' toads and frogs." He shook the rain from his hat and took off his slicker. "Ancy gave us a fine new heifer. Now, Kayla, tell me what happened. Who helped with the birthin'?"

"I did, Granpa. It happened so fast. I went out to see about Ancy before the storm hit, and before I knew it, I saw those little feet. I pulled, like I remember you did with the pigs."

He stood looking at her wide-eyed. "Well, I'll just be doggoned—you're sure one to reckon with. I'm proud of you." He chuckled and shook his head a few times. "You got yourself a fine calf."

"I sure 'nuf do. Can we go up now?" she asked.

Granpa looked at Gran. "You okay, Helen? You so quiet, woman."

"I got a pain in my chest, Vernell. Maybe gas." She stood up to follow him but changed her mind. She sighed again, and sat down on the rug and leaned against the beanbag.

"Let me dry off a bit, and I'll come help you." He went up the ladder.

"Bring my medicine—I don't think I better move yet." She rubbed her chest.

Kayla said, "I'll get it, Gran. Why didn't you tell me?" She started up the ladder.

"Nothin' unusual, child. I, oh . . ." Her voice trailed away.

Kayla saw Gran's eyes roll upwards. She yelled, "Granpa!" and scrambled up the ladder. She ran towards Gran's bedroom.

Uncle Walt was coming in from the storm, dripping water on the floor. Kayla screamed, "It's Gran! She's havin' some kind of attack! She needs the doctor!"

Uncle Walt picked up the phone as Granpa clambered down the ladder to the cellar.

"The line is dead!" exclaimed Uncle Walt. "I'll get the doctor!" He ran back out into the rainy darkness.

Kayla rushed down the ladder behind Granpa and held out the medicine and a cup of water.

Granpa leaned down and pinched Gran's nose and breathed into her mouth. Kayla held her breath while Granpa tried over and over to revive Gran. Kayla waited and waited, holding the water.

Finally Granpa cradled Gran in his arms.

"Helen's gone . . . gone," he whispered in a surprised voice. He looked confused. "She seemed fine when I came in. Didn't say a word."

"Granpa!" screamed Kayla, dropping the cup. "What you mean *gone?* She can't be gone that fast! Shake her, Granpa. She's just sleepin'!" She knelt down, sobbing, "Wake up, Gran! Wake up!"

Granpa put his arms around Kayla. They sat there on the floor for a long time.

Finally, Granpa said, "She's gone, honey girl. She's gone to heaven, gone to be with the angels." Tears rolled down his cheeks.

Kayla could hardly breathe. She looked at Gran's closed eyes and still face. "I want to die, too," she thought. "Gran will take me with her. We'll dance together—with the angels—Gran and me."

She heard the car door slam, footsteps on the porch. Someone was with Uncle Walt.

Someone was too late.

CHAPTER FIVE

The Train Ride

The wheels of the Amtrak grinding to a stop roused Kayla from her dream. It took a while for her to realize where she was. With her eyes still closed, she listened to sounds of people getting on and off the train. The conductor called, " 'Board!" She kept her eyes shut even as the train glided away from the station.

Kayla was so angry and confused. Aunt Martha said she would feel better if she could cry a little. As painful as it was, she refused, knowing it wouldn't bring Gran back. It wouldn't change having to go to Chicago to live with Aunt Martha. Crying hadn't brought Daddy home to see her for all these years, that was for sure. Finally, Kayla squinched one eye open and peeked out the window.

"Did you sleep okay?" Aunt Martha asked.

"Yes'm, I did." Kayla looked out into the early dawn. She sat up straight. Since leaving Washington,

D.C., the day before, they had gone through several mountain ranges. Kayla hadn't imagined anything near to what she now saw through the window. Gnarled and tangled trees grew so close to the track she could reach out and touch them as the train moved slowly over the pass. Brilliant-colored patches of wildflowers painted the gulches and hillsides.

Kayla allowed herself to smile. "I'm glad we saw part of the mountains. I won't forget how they look up close." She stood up. "Excuse me, Aunt Martha, I better go wash up a little bit."

"Okay, honey. Be sure to put paper on the seat, and remember to wash your hands. We can get some breakfast whenever you feel hungry."

When Kayla came out, the man she had seen last night was waiting. He smiled and nodded. She did not return his smile. His eyes were the same color as hers. She wondered if her daddy looked like him. Many times Gran had said, "That green-eyed devil, at least he could call or write you once in a while." When Kayla returned to her seat, Aunt Martha said, "You all right, Kayla? You look like you saw a ghost."

"Yes, Auntie, I'm okay." But she didn't feel okay.

She needed her daddy, and she didn't even know where to call him. She needed to tell him about Gran. Tears almost welled up in Kayla's eyes, but once again she held them back. Why had God let Gran die? It wasn't fair. Gran was the only mother she had known. "I will never say another prayer again," she told herself. "Never."

"Kayla," said Aunt Martha, as if reading her mind, "Mama had a long, healthy life. I know she wanted to go suddenly, like she did, rather than be sickly. I'll miss her, too. But death is a part of life. Try to remember the good things you did together. She would want it that way."

Kayla tried to listen, but it was no use. Gran was Aunt Martha's mother. Aunt Martha had a lifetime of good things to remember. Kayla did not want death to be a part of life. She did not want to *remember* Gran. She wanted to be with her.

"I know you wanted to stay with Granpa. But he thought it best you come to live with us."

"Why?" asked Kayla. "I could help out like I always did."

"Granpa thought you'd be too lonely by yourself. He will find somebody to help with the housework.

Just a year or so ago, Mama and I had discussed your coming to Chicago to go to junior high. We thought it would be good for you, even then."

Neither she nor Aunt Martha said anything for a long time. Kayla was glad. She couldn't imagine that going to Chicago would be good for her. She loved everything about the farm, and that's where she wanted to be. Did grownups always know what was best? They were wrong this time. She wanted to be with Granpa. There was nothing in Chicago for her.

Finally, Aunt Martha broke the silence. "I'm sorry we couldn't find your dad in time for the funeral."

Kayla touched her locket. "I wrote and told him about Gran, and that I was going to Chicago. His agent in New York sends his mail to wherever he is. That takes time, but I know he'll write me. And one day he'll come for me."

"I'm pretty sure he will," replied Aunt Martha. She smiled and patted Kayla's knee. "Don't worry. You'll like Chicago. Johnetta is looking forward to having a sister. Says she's sick to death of her brothers."

Aunt Martha pulled an envelope from her purse. "Here, let me show you her prom pictures." She handed snapshots to Kayla one at a time. "Her dress was lemon yellow, and she wore brown velvet accessories. What you think?"

Kayla looked at the slim, pretty girl with the short stylish haircut, posing next to a baby grand piano. She hadn't seen Johnetta for over two years and barely recognized her cousin—suddenly sixteen and grown-up. It was hard to imagine herself a little sister to this girl. "She's awful pretty; she looks like you. Is she a good piano player?"

"Oh yes, she plays a lot at school. She's a big help to the music teacher, and she plays for the young people's choir at church." Aunt Martha shuffled through the pictures and pulled out another one. "This is Hank in his baseball uniform, posing with your uncle Jerome. He's almost eighteen. That boy eats, sleeps, and breathes baseball. He and Aaron were named after your uncle's hero, Hank Aaron."

"I heard Granpa and Uncle Walt talk about him." said Kayla, trying to be polite.

"He's the ballplayer who broke Babe Ruth's home-run record back in 1974," explained Aunt Martha as she laid the pictures on the magazine she was reading.

"I read about Babe Ruth."

"Babe Ruth had been the world's baseball hero for so long it was hard for people to accept the fact that a black man broke his record. Matter of fact, before the game in 1974, Hank's life was threatened if he broke Babe's record of 714 home runs. Your uncle Jerome was in Atlanta; he actually saw Hank hit that 715th home run. He's never stopped talking about that game. At age forty-five, he still collects Hank Aaron cards and souvenirs."

"Really?" said Kayla. She didn't feel much like baseball talk, but she realized her aunt was trying to cheer her up. "I used to watch games with Granpa," said Kayla. "I don't remember many names."

Aunt Martha continued, as if thinking aloud, "Hank will be a junior this year. I hope he gets serious about a career soon. Hank Aarons are few and far between." She shuffled through the pictures again. "And this is Aaron. Remember him? He's ten. Loves video games. But currently, raising hamsters is his number one thing."

Listening to Aunt Martha talking about Aaron's pets made Kayla think about Balloo and Wilesy. How would they ever get along without her?

Aunt Martha squeezed Kayla's hand. "We'll be in Chicago before lunchtime, and Johnetta promised to fix a 'welcome-home' dinner for you." She opened the magazine she had been reading and flipped to find her page.

"Aunt Martha," began Kayla.

"What is it, dear?" Aunt Martha asked, looking up.

"Did you know my daddy?"

"Not really. I met him a couple of times when he and your mother passed through Chicago. He was very handsome. Your mom used to write me letters and postcards about him and the shows they danced in. Traveling all over the world must have been an exciting life. I have a few old snapshots of the two of them. Gosh, your mom was so excited when she found out she was pregnant with you! She wrote me from Africa about how she'd wanted a baby for so long. Then she got sick and had to come home. You know the rest, don't you?"

Kayla nodded.

"Granpa always says it was a miracle that you were born so healthy and smart," said Aunt Martha.

Kayla leaned against the seat. She thought about

Granpa, and the lump in her throat swelled. His eyes had filled with tears when he told her goodbye at the station. "It won't be nothin' here without you and your granma. But it's best you be with young people. An old man ain't enough to grow up with."

It was so awfully scary. Kayla closed her eyes and hugged Angel. Gran had made Angel when Kayla was a baby. She wasn't a pretty doll. But Kayla didn't believe that she was pretty herself—she was just ordinary, except for her green eyes. "Your face is interesting," Gran had said when kids teased Kayla about her cat eyes. "Anyway, it's what's inside that counts. And you dance like an angel, honey girl. You don't need to be movie-star pretty."

The train was slowing. Kayla saw houses and apartment buildings lining both sides of the tracks. Taller buildings of all sizes, colors, and shapes crowded the distance. No telling how many cities they had passed through since they left South Carolina, yet somehow she was sure that *this* was Chicago!

CHAPTER SIX

Chicago!

The conductor's voice came through the speaker, " 'Cawgo!"

Kayla felt a shiver run up her spine.

"We'll be at the station in a few minutes," Aunt Martha said. She started gathering her things. "You excited?"

"I'm a little scared."

Aunt Martha patted Kayla's shoulder. "I know, honey. And it's okay. But you'll love Chicago—everybody does."

Kayla heard the dragging and hissing of the engines as the train jerked to a final stop. The noise and confusion of passengers and porters pulling hand luggage from storage compartments filled the coach.

"Got your things together, Kayla?"

"Yes'm, I'm ready." She picked up her old blue

book bag. Inside were her most treasured possessions. A delicate pink Chantilly lace blouse and a pair of gold hoop earrings big around as a quarter fit into the cellophane bag from Aunt Martha's stockings. The blouse and earrings had belonged to her mother. Gran's black onyx comb, a necklace made from real African trading beads, and a small, cream-colored leather Bible folded inside a moss-green silk scarf were all wrapped in tissue paper, zipped in a freezer bag, and packed in one side of the book bag. She slipped her arms through the straps and picked up a small square suitcase the porter had taken down. With her free arm she grabbed Angel.

They got off the train, and Kayla kept up with Aunt Martha as she hurried to the terminal.

Ahead, a boy and girl were waiting. "There they are!" exclaimed Aunt Martha as the two started toward them.

Johnetta, complete with eye shadow and lipstick, looked just like her photo. She wore skin-tight faded jeans and a blue tee-shirt she had cut off so her midriff showed. Aaron's smooth, olive-colored face was shining clean. Otherwise, he looked like every other ten-year-old Kayla knew. He wore sloppy denim shorts, a Bulls tee-shirt, and dirty white gym shoes with no socks.

Johnetta and Aaron pounced upon Aunt Martha, hugging and kissing her.

Finally Johnetta hugged Kayla lightly and said softly, "I know you're going to miss Granma. I'm sorry I didn't see her more often." She held Kayla at arm's length for a few seconds. "So, you pretty tall for a *little* sister. Skinny, too, but we'll get you together." She hugged Kayla again.

Kayla said nothing, but she wondered what Johnetta meant about getting her together. She looked down at her denim skirt, blue cotton blouse, and new patent leather pumps. She knew she didn't look flashy or fancy, but she felt as together as she ever had. And why would Johnetta think she shouldn't be skinny, when she was so skinny herself?

Aaron was not as friendly. He studied her through huge brown eyes. "I'd rather have a boy cousin than a girl, but since you ain't trying to be fancy like most girls, I guess you'll be okay. Just stay outta my room and don't touch my stuff. Deal?" He stuck out his hand.

Kayla hesitated for a moment before she took it.

"Deal," she said. Aaron might be a pain, but he seemed to be honest.

Johnetta pushed Aaron's shoulder. "Shut up, Aaron! Try to be human, at least till we get home."

"Let's go," said Aunt Martha. She handed Johnetta two dollars. "Please get a cart, Johnetta—your dad is probably waiting."

Johnetta came back with the cart, and Aaron picked up Kayla's small suitcase. He yelled, "Whoa, whatcha got in this one, the family tree?"

"Books," said Kayla. "You too little to carry it?"

When she reached for it, he evaded her by swinging it around, almost losing his balance. He set it on the cart.

"Books? You weird or somethin'? School's out."

"Not schoolbooks, silly, my special books."

Johnetta said, "Grandma said you liked to read, but I'm not ready for a bookworm."

"Well, get ready," said Aunt Martha. "This bookworm is at the top of her class. Wait till you see her report cards. All A's."

After picking up the heavy luggage, they went outside and waited for Uncle Jerome in a huge driveway shaped like a horseshoe.

"He had to go out and 'round the block," said Aaron. "Here he comes!"

"I like your locket," Johnetta said to Kayla. "It's unusual. Is it antique?"

"I guess," replied Kayla. "Daddy sent it from Italy for my sixth birthday. It's my favorite thing—my lucky charm."

"So I can forget about borrowing it, huh?"

"I wear it all the time. Anyway, lucky charms can't be borrowed or loaned. They lose their power."

Johnetta chuckled. "Who told you that?"

"My friend Cammie. She doesn't even take her locket off at night."

A blue car pulled up to the curb. Uncle Jerome jumped out and kissed Aunt Martha. "Hi, honey, how was the trip?"

"What can I say? It wasn't easy," said Aunt Martha. "But everything went as well as could be expected. Uncle Walt will move in with Granpa. They'll find someone to help with the cooking and cleaning."

Kayla hadn't remembered that her uncle was so tall and handsome. He picked her up and hugged her warmly. "My, my, you grew up since we saw you,

Kayla. How long has it been, Martha, two or three years?"

"Two and a half years," said Aunt Martha. "We visited at Christmas, remember?"

"How fast the time goes by!"

After stacking the bags in the trunk, they all got in the car and drove out of the station. Kayla had never been in such a fancy car. "They must be pretty rich," she thought.

"Where's Hank?" asked Aunt Martha. "He promised to be here when I came home." When no one answered, Aunt Martha turned to Uncle Jerome. "Well, where is he?"

"He's playing ball over at the park. Last game before the playoffs," Uncle Jerome said quietly.

"But he promised to be here to meet Kayla. Baseball is not all there is in life."

Kayla looked out the window and tried to enjoy the ride. She really didn't mind that Hank hadn't come to meet her. Aaron and Johnetta were enough. There would be time to meet Hank later. She liked Uncle Jerome immediately and wondered if her own daddy looked anything like him. How lucky Johnetta was to have a wonderful mother and a father who was there when she needed him! Already she felt jealous of her pretty cousin.

They all talked at once, and nobody listened to what anybody said. Trying to see the city and hear the conversation was not easy. Kayla leaned back against the seat and looked out the window. She had never seen such tall, important-looking buildings. As they drove along the shore of the seemingly endless lake, she almost forgot about the ache in her throat.

Uncle Jerome turned away from the lake and drove through one crowded street after another. At last he pulled up in front of a solid-looking red brick bungalow trimmed in white. "Welcome home, Kayla," he said.

Kayla looked at her new home. "It's not fancy," she thought. "But it looks sure of itself."

She followed Johnetta up the steps and into the living room. Hot as it was outside, it was nice and cool inside. "Air-conditioning," she thought. A rose-colored sofa and two matching tapestry chairs were grouped in front of the fireplace. Family pictures crowded the mantel. She noticed the baby grand piano and said to Johnetta, "Aunt Martha told me you play the piano. I bet that's cool."

"I play a little," said Johnetta.

"I'm going to be a ballet dancer," said Kayla.

"Really? That's ambitious," said Johnetta.

"I danced in the school musicals. Last Christmas I danced by myself and got three curtain calls." Kayla stopped. They were all staring at her. She felt her face burn with embarrassment.

"Well, do-oot, what you say?" hooted Aaron sarcastically.

"Hush, Aaron," said Johnetta. "C'mon, I'll show you the bedroom." She picked up the two large bags, and Kayla carried the rest of her things. As they went by the kitchen, Johnetta said, "Mom and Dad's room is on the other side." At the end of the hall were two doors. "The middle door goes to the back porch," she explained, "and the one to the left goes to the attic and Hank's room. It also leads to the basement, where Aaron keeps his hamsters. I advise you to avoid both at all costs."

Kayla followed Johnetta into a short hallway; at the end she could see the bathroom. Johnetta pushed open a door to the left and nodded her head. "That's Aaron's bedroom across the hall." A sign on his door read, ALL WHO ENTER ARE DOOMED!

Johnetta set the bags down and spread her arms dramatically. "This is it, cousin. That's your bed over by that window. I'm afraid you'll have to live out of your suitcase till the chest we ordered gets delivered. There's not enough space in mine for a roach to hide. We'll share the dresser. By the time you start wearing makeup and needing mirror time, I hope to be out of here."

Kayla stood holding her bags. The room was pretty. The twin beds had matching floral comforters with white lace skirts. The white mini-blinds were draped with matching flowered valances.

Suddenly Kayla thought of her room at home. She began to tremble, and her eyes filled with tears. She was going to cry, and she couldn't stop it. She fell on the bed and sobbed.

She cried for Gran whose arms would never again comfort her. She cried for Granpa who would be missing Gran so much. She was vaguely aware of Johnetta closing the door. All the tears she had held back for so long came pouring out, and she cried and cried, just for herself.

CHAPTER SEVEN

The Locket

After a long time, just when Kayla was feeling exhausted enough to fall asleep, Aaron poked his head in the door. "I wouldn't cry if I was you," he said. "Makes you u-g-l-y."

Johnetta came up and pushed the door open. She slapped his behind. "Pest! Get out of here!" She sucked her teeth like Gran used to do. "He gets better as time goes by, or at least you'll get used to him, I hope."

She handed Kayla a glass. "Here, have a slug of lemonade. Maybe you want to take a shower before dinner since you rode on the train all day and night. There's a little blue terry robe hanging in the closet space I made for you; towels are in the hall linen closet. Help yourself. Hope you like roast pork and oven fries. I also baked some apples with brown sugar." She went out and closed the door.

Kayla sipped the cold, sweet lemonade. She felt better. She took clean clothes out of her suitcase and slipped on the soft robe. She realized the lump in her throat was gone for the first time since Gran died. "Gosh," she said, "I'm hungry as a big dog." She showered and dressed quickly so they wouldn't have to wait for her.

Hank came home as they sat down to eat. His clothes were dirty, but he was tall and good-looking like his dad. He had light brown eyes and a chipped front tooth, which made his smile seem more friendly. He kissed her lightly on the forehead. "Excuse my sweat, Kayla. Welcome to our humble abode." Aaron crossed his eyes. Hank kissed his mother and said, "Man, am I glad you're back. Johnetta's cooking can get pretty darn boring."

"Go wash up, Hank," said Aunt Martha. "You're lucky she cooked anything at all for you."

Johnetta shrugged. "Hank has no taste. He'd be happy with pizza and chocolate cake every day. If you ask me, that's zitsville."

"I don't get zits," said Aaron smugly.

"You're not grown-up enough," called Hank as he headed to the bathroom. "Zits pick on men who can take 'em."

"I think you did very well planning the meals, Johnetta," said Uncle Jerome. "I enjoyed every last one." He sliced more roast and served the plates.

"C'mon, Dad," piped up Aaron. "All that jello?"

Johnetta said, "I only made jello three times."

"But we had it left over *four* times," complained Aaron. "We even had green jello, and I *hate* green jello."

Kayla said, "Well, dinner is really good tonight, Johnetta. Everything tastes delicious. Green is my favorite jello, Aaron."

"So?" He looked at her. "Well, you eat it from now on, all of it."

"Aaron, don't be rude," said Uncle Jerome.

Hank returned to the table and sat next to his mother. "You promised to meet us at the station," she said to him.

"I know, Ma, and I'm sorry, but I couldn't miss this game. I'm sure Kayla understands."

Aunt Martha sighed. "How is your practice coming along?"

"I thought you'd never ask. I'm big-time now. I made starting pitcher."

"That's great, son," said Uncle Jerome. "Think you're ready to take on the responsibility? Just remember our talk about summer school. I wasn't joking. No baloney! Your studies come first."

"I know, Dad. I'll take care of business from now on, for real."

Aunt Martha said, "I hope you mean that, Hank. You were lucky they were offering the math class this summer. You may not be that lucky another time."

Kayla looked around at her new family. How would she ever get to know them? How would she know what to say? Listening to the talk around the dinner table made her feel so lonely and shy. She wondered what it would be like to sit at a table like this with her daddy. She wished Gran and Granpa were there, or Cheefus. She wished *all* of them were there. She wrapped her hand around her locket.

Aaron turned to Johnetta, "What's for dessert, Sis?"

Johnetta smiled her sweetest smile, "Green jello, twerp." She winked at Kayla. Then she went to the kitchen and brought out a delicious-looking cobbler. "Peach!" she announced.

"My favorite dessert!" said Kayla.

"Peach cobbler is everybody's favorite dessert," said Aaron.

Uncle Jerome laughed. "You may be right, Aaron. In all my years, I've never run across *anybody* who didn't like it."

After dinner, Aaron said, "C'mon, Kayla, I've got a new video game."

Kayla hesitated. "I'm prob'ly not too good. I haven't played many video games. Anyway, I should help with the dishes."

"No," said Aunt Martha. "You're excused your first night here. Go on and play."

Kayla caught on fast. Aaron grumbled when she made a bad play, but she could tell he was impressed. At eight-thirty, Kayla was ready for bed. She fell asleep at once. She didn't even hear her cousin come in.

Kayla's chest-of-drawers was delivered early the next day. She spent the morning unpacking and organizing her things neatly in the drawers. She put Stephanie Dabney's photo on top of her chest, along with pictures of her mother, Gran, and Granpa. She unrolled her dance poster and showed it to Johnetta. Johnetta said, "Hey, girl, it's beautiful. Autographed yet. Hang it on the wall between the windows. You ought to get a frame for it."

"I will," said Kayla.

Johnetta lowered her voice. "I've got a date, but don't tell. Mom doesn't like the guy I'm going with. Thinks he's too old. He's only nineteen. He says he likes me because I'm mature for my age. Tyree is *so* cool."

Kayla looked at Johnetta for a few seconds thinking, but not saying, "Uh-oh, that sounds like trouble."

After lunch, Johnetta said, "Mom, if it's okay, I'm going to a movie with Jen and Kramaria. It's Jen's birthday."

Aunt Martha picked up the skirt she was hemming. "Well, it's not okay. Aaron went swimming, and it's Kayla's first day here. I'm sure she doesn't want to watch me sew."

"Aw, Mom, I promise to get back early. I'd take her with but... well, you know."

Kayla said, "I'm gonna write some letters, and I

got things to do myself. So just act like I'm not here."

"Thanks, Kayla. I owe you one," said Johnetta. "Is it okay, Mom?"

Aunt Martha gave in. "Well, I guess. But be back before dinner."

"Gotcha." Johnetta ran out of the room and down the hall.

Aunt Martha sighed. "I hope you don't mind doing your own thing today, Kayla—Johnetta does have a busy life. Just make yourself at home. You might want to go out and sit in the sun while I finish sewing. If you need anything, yell."

"Thanks, Aunt Martha. Don't worry 'bout me, I can find plenty to do."

Kayla decided to go outside. The tiny backyard and Aunt Martha's flower garden were so pretty. Gran had taught her the names of most of the flowers. There were marigolds, zinnias, baby's breath, and red roses. She remembered the day in early spring when she had helped Gran plant her flowers. Gran had pink roses—Kayla's favorite. For a long time Kayla sat on a large rock among the flowers, thinking about her grandmother and the farm.

After a while she went inside. She could hear the hum of Aunt Martha's sewing machine. Even though Johnetta had warned her about Aaron's menagerie, she was curious. She opened the door leading to the basement. A night-light at the bottom of the steps cast eerie little circles on the wall. She wondered if anybody's ghost hung around down there. Cautiously, she went down the stairs.

To the right, a small window let in enough light for her to see. The door on the left was closed. She opened it and peered in. The room was dark, except for a small window with cages in front of it. She couldn't find a light switch. Little rustling sounds came from the cages.

Piano music from above distracted her. Johnetta must be back—her date hadn't lasted long. Kayla decided to postpone further investigation of the basement, and she ran upstairs to watch Johnetta practice. She was impressed. Johnetta played quite well, and Kayla listened for twenty minutes or more before reluctantly going to the kitchen to help Aunt Martha with dinner.

When they finished eating, Aunt Martha said, "Kayla, you should go around the block and see the neighborhood. Aaron, take your cousin for a walk before it gets dark."

"Do I have to?" whined Aaron.

"Or die," said Johnetta. She winked at Kayla as she scraped the dishes and put them in the dishwasher.

"Do I have to say she's my cousin?" he wanted to know.

"That would be nice," said Aunt Martha. "She is, you know. Whatever you call her, just be nice. And no funny business, you hear?"

"Oh, all right. Come on," he mumbled to Kayla. "I was hoping you wouldn't be any trouble. Here I am having to take care of you already."

"I'll make it up to you," said Kayla. She followed him out the back door. "One of these days you may need me."

"For what? What good are girls anyway?"

"You'll see." She followed him down the steps and out the gate, trying to memorize everything she saw. At the end of the alley they turned and headed to the corner.

"C'mon," Aaron said impatiently. "The school's two blocks away. If we run, maybe none of my friends will see us." He waited for her to catch up, then pointed ahead. "That's the park over there, where we skate and play ball after school. Let's go." They took off and ran two long blocks until he stopped in front of a sprawling three-story school with a chain-link fence around it. "There it is."

Kayla's mouth fell open. "Gosh, it's pretty big," she said, thinking of the ten-room school in South Carolina.

"Not as big as where Johnetta and Hank go. The high school is *really* big."

They walked around the building. Kayla's stomach felt a little wiggly. Across the alley, behind an apartment building, she could see beautiful slashes of orange, pink, and purple in the blue sky. A lonely feeling overtook her, and for a moment, all the city noises seemed to stop. In the quiet, she could hear Gran saying, "I miss you, too, honey girl. I do miss you."

The sound of a nearby siren brought Kayla out of her reverie. She was standing near the fence by herself. Aaron was nowhere in sight.

She ran to the end of the school and looked down the next street. Aaron was gone. She tried to stay calm. She knew she could find her way back home—it was just a couple of blocks.

She ran to the next corner and looked in both directions. Still no Aaron.

Two boys came out of an apartment building across the street. They stood looking at her, then they crossed the street and came right up to her. One boy, who wore a blue baseball cap and dark glasses, blocked her way. "Hey, sister, how much money you got?"

"None." She tried to walk around them, and he stepped in front of her.

The other boy, who had sandy-colored braids, stood watching. Frowning, he said, "C'mon man, leave her go."

The boy in the baseball cap ignored his friend. "What you mean none?" he said to Kayla. "You ain't got a dollar?"

"No," said Kayla.

He reached over and grabbed her braid and pulled her head to one side. He yanked her locket off her neck. "This will do for now. You better have some cash money next time I see you."

Kayla screamed, "No!"

The boys ran across the street, past the school, and around the corner. For a moment Kayla just stood still, stunned. Then the horrible realization that her locket was gone overtook her. "I'll die without my locket. I'll just *die!*" she thought. She ran down the sidewalk—two long blocks—and up the front steps of her new home. She pushed the doorbell several times, then pounded on the door.

At last Aunt Martha opened the door. "Gracious, Kayla, what's the matter? Where's Aaron?"

"He left me," said Kayla angrily. "He left me, and two boys blocked my way. One of them took my locket, 'cause I didn't have a dollar!" Tears streamed down her face.

"Oh, no!" Aunt Martha put her arms around her niece. "Honey, I'm so sorry. Where is that Aaron? I'll call the police. Tell me what they look like." She picked up the phone and dialed the number.

Johnetta had come out of the kitchen. "Gosh, Kayla, what a horrible thing to happen! I hope you weren't scared to death." She hugged Kayla. "They're just punks who realized you're new in the neighborhood. Once they know you, they won't bother you. Aaron is a stinker for leaving you."

"Somebody call me?" asked Aaron as he came in the back door. "Where'd you go, Kayla? You were looking at the sunset, so I went to say hi to Jimmy. Came back and you had split."

"Why did you leave Kayla, Aaron? Go to your room and stay there for the rest of the evening," said Aunt Martha.

Aaron looked surprised. "Why... I—"

"Just go. You were thoughtless and inconsiderate." Into the phone she said, "Yes, Sergeant, I want to report a robbery."

Kayla described the boys, and Aunt Martha repeated the description. "About thirteen or fourteen. African-American. The one who took the necklace was medium brown, chubby. He was wearing a red shirt, a blue baseball cap, and sunglasses. The other one was lighter-skinned with braids—also wearing sunglasses... shorts... blue-and-white gyms... Yes, both of them."

Kayla sank down on the sofa. Her only real connection to Daddy, gone. Mama's picture, gone. She rubbed the place on her chest where the locket had lain for what seemed like most of her life. It had always been her special comfort, even when Gran was alive. Why would the boys even want it? It was a joke to them, but it had been everything to her.

"You want something to drink?" asked Johnetta.

"No, thanks," murmured Kayla.

Oh, why had she come to Chicago? This would never have happened back on the farm. She stared absently at the television as *Wheel of Fortune* came on. Once again, a lump rose in her throat.

CHAPTER EIGHT

Kayla's New Family

The next morning Kayla moped around her room, soaking herself in her sorrow. At lunch she picked at her food. The day after she had no appetite for anything except a hot dog. Every day that week Aunt Martha made her a grilled hot dog on a toasted bun for lunch. Johnetta complained, but Aaron and Hank loved them. One day Hank brought her a Mr. Goodbar. "This is everybody's favorite candy bar," he said. "If you can't eat this, I'm calling in the medics, 'cause you are sure 'nuf sick!"

Kayla smiled weakly. "It's my favorite, too, Hank. Thanks."

In the afternoons, Aunt Martha coaxed her into the garden. Kayla mostly just sat in the sun while Aunt Martha took care of her flowers and chatted away. "You know, I used to help Mama with her garden. I have almost every kind of flower she loved right here. I helped on the farm, too—fed the chickens and milked the cows. That was okay, but I hated picking cotton!"

Kayla found out that not much had changed on the farm since Aunt Martha grew up there. It made her feel closer to her aunt since they had such shared experiences, but she missed Gran even more.

Aunt Martha made her get up every day and go through the motions of living. Kayla made her bed and helped with the cleaning and laundry. After dinner, while doing the dishes, she listened to Johnetta chatter about everything—including her secret meetings with Tyree. Kayla found this mildly interesting. She really liked Johnetta and hoped she knew what she was doing.

Three weeks went by. One day early in July, Kayla was cleaning the bathroom when Aunt Martha called, "Who wants to go shopping?"

"I do! I need some stuff for my animals," yelled Aaron.

"How 'bout you, Kayla? It'll do you good to get out and see the neighborhood. You might enjoy it."

"Okay, I'll go, Aunt Martha." She finished picking up the bathroom. It was full of Aaron's stuff. A room looked like a tornado had struck it after he left it. With an armload of clothes, she knocked on his door. "Do these by any chance belong to you?" she asked innocently.

He peered at the tee-shirt and shorts as if he'd never seen them before. Suddenly, he grabbed them. "What you doing with my things? I been looking all over for them. Ma, Kayla's stealing my stuff already!"

"Yeah, sure, like I want your wormy clothes. Plus, you left a ring in the bathtub."

"If I didn't leave the ring, how could you tell I bathed?"

Aunt Martha came down the hall. "C'mon, you two, if you're going. I've got a lot to do."

Kayla pulled Aunt Martha's folding shopping cart. They walked for several blocks, passing the school and two churches.

Tucked between apartment buildings and storefronts were houses of all kinds and colors, some poking their porches or stoops practically onto the sidewalk. Some had small gardens with fences and wrought-iron gates. They passed a resale shop where a used tape recorder in the window caught Kayla's eye. A bookstore had new and used books, dolls, and knickknacks of every kind. Soon they were walking by more stores and restaurants. Delicious smells drifted out onto the street. Kayla noticed that all kinds of people seemed to live in the neighborhood.

"There's a pet store," said Aaron. "I need cages for my baby hamsters when they're born. They should come today or tomorrow."

Aunt Martha said, "Okay. Kayla, go with Aaron, please, and when you're finished, you two wait in front. I'll run across the street to the bakery."

In the pet store, an enormous red-bearded man standing behind the counter frowned as they came in. He laid the last piece of a candy bar on the counter as he said, "What you kids want?"

Kayla felt a little nervous. She wondered if the man spoke that rudely to everybody or if it was because they were kids, and maybe, because they were black.

"You got any baby hamster cages?" asked Aaron.

"I got hamster cages. You can put babies in if you want to." He picked up the candy and stuffed it in his mouth, then went to a shelf stacked with cages of different sizes and shapes. Kayla and Aaron followed him. "Let you have this one for twelve dollars." He selected a small round wire cage.

"That's too much," said Aaron. "I bought one just like it from another store for eight dollars."

"Take it or leave it," growled the man as he walked back to the counter. Under his breath he added, "Doggone kids, always wanting something for nothing."

"We do not!" said Kayla, putting her hand on Aaron's shoulder. "We have money; you're trying to cheat us. C'mon, Aaron, we'll spend our money where we're welcome."

"Just a minute—which one of you took my candy bar?" He came from behind the counter and stood looking down on them.

"You ate it," said Kayla.

"I put a whole candy bar on the counter—right here." He pounded the counter with his massive fist. "Pay up!" He held out a fat hand.

Aaron stood with his mouth open.

Kayla pushed Aaron out of the man's reach, and they ran out of the store.

"Colored kids—you're all thieves!" he yelled at them.

They met Aunt Martha and told her what had

happened. She was furious. "I'll report him to the Better Business Bureau. The *nerve* of him, calling you thieves."

"At least he knows all kids aren't dummies about what things cost," said Kayla. "Aaron told him!"

"I hope you never go into that store again," her aunt said.

"The candy bar is what bugged me," said Aaron. "Tryin' to accuse us of stealing the germy candy he had slobbered on—yuk!" He looked at Kayla. "I'm glad you went in with me, Kayla. He coulda made mincemeat outta me."

"Right," teased Kayla, "and fed you to his animals."

"Kayla!" admonished Aunt Martha.

"Sorry, just kiddin'," said Kayla. "I'm glad I was there, too, Aaron. But what about your cage?"

"I can use a box until Dad can pick one up for me."

"Last stop will be to get a few groceries," said Aunt Martha. "And I think you both need a treat."

They bought frozen custard cones. While walking home on the crowded street, Kayla touched Aunt Martha's arm. "Thanks for making me come,

Auntie. It was fun seeing all the shops."

When they got home, Kayla helped put the groceries away. Aunt Martha bought interesting things like yogurt and sunflower seeds and microwave popcorn. Back on the farm, Kayla ate buttermilk curds she had churned; pumpkin seeds she had dug out of pumpkins, dried, and roasted; and popcorn from the cob. Granpa always planted popcorn between the pumpkins and watermelons.

Kayla thought about what the man in the pet shop had said. "Colored kids—you're all thieves." No one had ever said anything like that to her before. It made her feel a little sick to her stomach. She asked Aunt Martha, "Why was that man so mean?"

"Could be he's prejudiced," said Aunt Martha. "He judges people before he gets to know them. He didn't like you and Aaron even before you went into his store."

"He didn't give us a chance to be nice."

"Don't worry about it, honey. There was nothing you could have done."

"I guess," said Kayla. She picked up her writing tablet, went out to the garden, and sat on the big rock.

She wrote:

Dear Daddy,

I went shopping with Aunt Martha today. It was an interesting experience. I' d sure like to talk to you about it when I see you. I'm beginning to feel like Chicago is home. I still miss Gran and Granpa awfully but Aunt Martha says it will get better as time goes by. She's good to me, and we get along great. I hope that you will come soon.

Love and XXX,

Kayla

She addressed the envelope and licked her last stamp. Was Daddy even getting her letters? He must not be. If he knew about Gran, he would have written or come. It was a sure thing her letters were stacked up somewhere waiting for him to pick them up.

CHAPTER NINE

A Place to Dance

The back door opened, and Aaron stuck his head out.

"Wanna see my new baby hamsters? They don't stay new long."

"Sure," Kayla replied. She gathered up her tablet and letter and followed Aaron to the basement.

"See?" He pointed to a pile of newspaper litter and the mother hamster inside a big cage.

Kayla peered in and saw four or five hairless critters about the size of her thumb. "They're not too cute yet. They look just like mice."

"Don't you know nothin'? They're the same family as mice. They'll be ready to mate in forty-five to sixty days."

"For real?" said Kayla. "You must have hamsters coming out your ears. Do you sell them?"

"Naah, I give 'em away to anybody who wants

one. See?" He picked up a hand-lettered sign that read, BABY HAMSTERS FOR FREE. "The minute they're weaned, they're outta here."

"I bet you could sell them."

Kayla looked around the basement. Old furniture and boxes filled one side of the huge room, but on the other side there was a large empty space—enough room for dancing! "Wow, you're lucky to have a place this big all to yourself."

"Boys need a private place to work in," said Aaron.

How nice it would be to have some space to dance! Kayla decided she'd wait until she knew Aaron better before asking him if she could practice here.

"See, I took the daddy hamster out and put him over here. He may get a little jealous of the babies when the mama don't pay him any attention. Wanna hold him?"

Kayla held out her hand and took the furry animal. "Oh, he's so soft!" She watched Aaron put fresh litter in the cage.

Suddenly he looked up. "You know that first day, I knew you could find your way home. But I hadn't counted on somebody taking your necklace and scaring you—honest."

"I wasn't scared, just mad."

"Well, I woulda been scared. Mostly it's pretty safe around here, but I guess you never can tell when bad guys are gonna show up."

Kayla hadn't thought about Aaron being just a little kid who could be scared himself. Here he was apologizing as best he could. Suddenly her shoulders felt lighter, and some of the funny feeling in her stomach eased up.

Upstairs, Johnetta was playing the piano. Kayla said, "Thanks for showing me the babies, Aaron. They're really neat." She put the hamster in its cage and ran upstairs to listen.

When the piece ended, Kayla clapped enthusiastically. Johnetta smiled. "Want to learn how to play a song, cousin? Come sit on the bench." She moved over to make room and showed Kayla how to play "Kumbaya." "It's an African song," she explained.

Kayla learned it quickly. Johnetta said, "Hey, maybe you ought to learn how to read music."

"We learned the lines and spaces and basic

rhythms at school," said Kayla.

Talking about music made her realize she hadn't danced in a long time. How could she be ready to dance with Daddy if she didn't keep up her practicing? In the confusion of leaving the farm with Aunt Martha, she had even forgotten to bring her two dance records. She needed to find a way to dance, maybe even take dance lessons. She missed Gran and Granpa and Cheefus, but she missed dancing, too. Dancing had always made her feel alive and happy.

Johnetta sorted through her music books and pulled out an old one. She taught Kayla a few more songs. She said, "I have to admit, cousin, you do catch on fast."

The next day, when Aaron was out with a friend, Kayla decided to try her luck at dancing in the basement. She headed down to the space where Aaron had his hamsters. Among the pieces of furniture was an old-fashioned dresser with a huge mirror. She pushed it into the open space and tilted the mirror until it reflected her whole body. She curtsied and did a little dance, then proceeded to practice her jetés and turns.

It was wonderful to be dancing again. All she needed was music. Gran used to say, "If you want it bad enough, and it's sensible, you can find a way."

The next morning Johnetta said, "I'm going to the resale shop. Wanna go?"

"Sure," said Kayla. "Shall I take my money?"

"I guess. You may find something you can't live without."

The used tape player was still in the window. It could be the solution to her music problem! It cost $29.95. She had saved twenty-five dollars, and her allowance from Granpa was five dollars a week. She could afford it! She couldn't get ballet slippers right away, but music was more important.

When she told Johnetta her plan, her cousin said, "Sounds like a dumb move to me, spending all your money on a tape player just to dance by. You're not really serious about dancing, are you Kayla? C'mon, get a grip."

At dinner that night, Aunt Martha was more sympathetic. She said, "If that's your dream, it's worth the sacrifice."

Aaron said, "I saw where you cleared a space in the basement. If you think I'm gonna listen to music and watch you dance around all the time, you're nuts. You'll make my animals nervous."

"I'll try hard not to bother you and your animals," said Kayla.

Uncle Jerome cut into his apple pie. "Try to remember, Aaron, Kayla is not a visitor. She is a member of this family, and she has as much right to dance as you have to keep your hamsters. You'll have to give a little and not be so selfish." He smiled at Kayla. "Furthermore, she may become famous one day and you can say, 'Hey, I shared my space with her!' "

Aaron looked down at his plate, and everybody was quiet. Finally, Kayla said, "Maybe I can find a cheaper tape player."

"Twenty-nine dollars is pretty cheap already," said Hank. "The best for your money is the smart move. I'll try to keep an eye open for something good."

"Gosh, Hank, thanks a lot," Kayla said.

After that, Kayla noticed when Aaron went to tend his animals. She would go down and pet the hamsters and talk to him. He knew a lot about his animals, and she was a good listener. One day she said, "Maybe you should show me how to clean the cages in case you need me to do it sometime."

"Okay," he said. "But that's not gonna happen." Just the same, he showed her how to clean the cages and give the hamsters their food. And when he wasn't there, she used his radio and danced to any music she could find. He pretended not to know—at least he didn't say anything. She appreciated that.

Kayla hadn't been to church since Gran's funeral. She just hadn't felt like it, and Aunt Martha had not insisted. But one Sunday in August there was a graduation program for the preschool kids who were going into kindergarten. Johnetta was going to play the piano. Kayla didn't want to miss seeing her.

She woke up suddenly as Johnetta came into the room fresh from her shower. Kayla said, "Why didn't you wake me? We don't want to be late."

Johnetta stood at the dresser and took the curlers out of her hair. "Church doesn't begin until eleven o'clock."

"But don't you have to be there early?"

"Relax. We've got time."

Kayla took a quick shower and dressed.

After breakfast, everybody piled into the car. It was too hot to walk. But even though there was no air-conditioning in the church, people were all dressed up. The little girls participating in the program wore matching dresses made out of beautiful black-and-white African fabric. The boys' shirts were made from the same fabric. One of the teachers had made all the clothes. The children looked very festive.

The program began with Johnetta playing while the congregation sang, "Lift Every Voice and Sing." Next, the children told what they wanted to be when they grew up. Then Johnetta played again, and each child sang a verse made up to the tune of "This Little Light of Mine." The children were given certificates of achievement. At the end everyone sang, "I Believe I Can Fly." That was the best part for Kayla. She sang along, "I believe I can touch the sky."

Being in church reminded Kayla of Sundays with Gran and Granpa. She missed singing along with them. They knew all the hymns from memory. She loved Granpa's loud, deep voice.

The minister prayed for a long time when the children finished singing. Kayla listened, but somehow praying wasn't the same as it used to be. She wondered if feeling thankful for her new family was the same as praying. It was a question she could have asked Gran. Perhaps she would have to ask Aunt Martha about it sometime.

CHAPTER TEN

School Daze

School opened September fourth. The thought of going to a new school and not knowing a soul was really scary. It was still hot, so Kayla wore her new red shorts and a white tee. As she got ready, she thought about her lost locket. She'd never gone to school without it. She didn't feel completely dressed. She threw a kiss to Angel and whispered, "Wish me luck."

Mrs. Giles, her homeroom teacher, was tall and regal and serious-looking. She assigned seats and handed out books to rowdy, excited kids, but remained cool herself, never even raising her voice. Kayla liked her immediately.

"Kayla, since you're new to Chicago, would you like to tell us a little about yourself?" Mrs. Giles asked her when everyone had settled down.

Kayla stood up. "I am from Blaner, South

Carolina. I grew up on a farm there with my granpa and granma. My granpa and uncle Walt started a farm co-op twenty years ago. People who belong help each other and share farm equipment. My friend Cheefus and I liked to fish in the creek. I am going to be a ballet dancer when I grow up." Her face grew hot.

She sat down and studied her hands. At first there was absolute quiet, then a few giggles and whisperings. Mrs. Giles said, "Thank you, Kayla, that's interesting. I'd like to know more about the farm co-op. I wish you'd write a short report and tell us about it." She called on someone else.

By the time everybody finished telling about summer vacations, the bell rang. The kids scrambled for their lockers, and Kayla followed the crowd to her next class.

A tall, thin boy with thick glasses caught up with her. "My brother told me that the first day is the worst. Better leave your books in your locker between classes—they get kinda heavy."

He was right. In fifth grade, she had been in a self-contained classroom, in a small school; here, the school was big and exciting, with all kinds of kids—

black, white, Asian, Hispanic. It was different, and she would have to get used to it. Changing rooms for each subject was just one new thing.

In math class, she flipped through her book with rising interest. It had a wonderful, clean, brand-new smell. This was the first time she could remember having a math book no one else had used before. She wished she could show her book to Gran. Kayla had always made A's in math back in South Carolina, and Gran used to brag about it to her church friends.

At lunch, Kayla used some of her allowance to buy a slice of pizza and a can of orange pop. She sat with four girls who practically ignored her. They talked to each other about summer vacation. They whispered behind their hands and giggled a lot. One girl, named Carlese, always looked as if she was smelling something unpleasant. Kayla studied the girls and wondered if any one of them would become her friend.

By the end of the first week, Kayla knew her way around the building, and she was getting used to her teachers. The tall boy with glasses, whose name she learned was Jesse King, spoke whenever he saw her.

But she really hadn't made a friend. At lunchtime, she ate quietly by herself.

She missed Cammie and the fun they had had in fifth grade. After school, she went right home and straight to the basement to practice dancing. She still hadn't bought a tape player; Hank hadn't had time to look. So she found the best music she could on Aaron's radio.

On Monday, Jesse brought an eighteen-inch garter snake for the class terrarium. Kayla picked it up. "Pretty cool for a girl, not being scared of a snake and all," Jesse said.

"What's to be scared of?" asked Kayla. "It's just a garter snake. They won't hurt you. We used to catch them all the time down on the farm."

"Yes, but the other girls are scared to touch it," Jesse pointed out.

"I am not scared," said Jerdine. "I just don't *like* touching any old snake."

"Me, neither," said Carlese. "I think Kayla's just showing off. Thinks she's braver than we are. I don't think she's so cool."

"It ain't brave, Carlese. I happen to know they won't hurt you."

"Just country, if you ask me," said Carlese. "And the word is *isn't,* not *ain't.*" She sniffed and turned up her nose.

Kayla felt like slapping her. Carlese closed her eyes and lifted her chin, then flipped her loosely curling hair over her shoulder. It was perfect hair, Kayla had to admit—not too curly, not too straight—probably because one of her parents was black and the other was white. Kayla shrugged her shoulders and went to her seat.

At home, she asked Johnetta why the girls weren't friendly. "I'm not that cute and my clothes aren't that great. They couldn't be jealous. They stand in little groups and giggle when I come around."

"You're all going through a weird age," said Johnetta. "Give 'em time. I promise you'll have more friends than you need by Christmas."

"At least flinging my hair around like Carlese is one thing I can't do to get attention. She looks silly. I wouldn't do it even if I could."

Johnetta ran her fingers through her own relaxed curly hair. "You don't need to be jealous. White girls want their hair to look naturally curly and kinky.

Is Carlese white?"

"No! And I am *not* jealous!" Kayla felt her face get warm.

"You could save your money, and get a perm to relax your hair," Johnetta suggested. "But they're kind of expensive to maintain. And your braids are okay, you know."

The next day at school, Kayla studied Carlese and thought, "I don't want her to think I want my hair like hers. I won't get a perm. I like skinny braids—that's what I want—skinny braids like Stephanie Dabney has."

After science class, a girl named Cynthia came up to Kayla. "I was scared of the snake 'til you picked it up, Kayla. I think you're brave. I touched it today. I wouldn't know that snakes feel cold and soft if I hadn't touched it." She smiled.

Kayla had never had a white friend before, but she looked into Cynthia's blue eyes and knew they would become friends. She said, "Thanks, Cynthia."

Mrs. Giles had been watching and listening to the kids talk about the snake. Finally she said, "Okay, boys and girls, take your seats and settle down."

Jesse raised his hand, and she nodded in his direction.

"I plan to be a zoologist and handle snakes, Mrs. Giles. I caught at least ten snakes last summer in Lincoln Park."

"That's great, Jesse. I was going to ask for a volunteer to do a report on snakes, and you are obviously the person for the job because of your real interest."

Kayla raised her hand, and Mrs. Giles called on her.

"When will you let the snake go?"

Mrs. Giles said, "Jesse, can you answer that?"

"Oh, we'll keep it and watch it shed its skin next spring," said Jesse.

Kayla's eyes widened. "That's cruel," she said. "How would you like to be trapped in a glass cage for the whole winter?"

Jesse's face darkened a little. "Snakes are different. They're cold-blooded, and they don't have feelings like other animals."

"But they're part of our environment," said Kayla. "Plus, how you do know they don't have feelings?"

Several kids laughed out loud.

Jessie frowned. "How can we study them if we don't capture them? They may have a better life in captivity—at least they don't get killed living in zoos."

Kayla was not convinced that snakes should be kept in cages, but since Mrs. Giles said nothing, she had to give Jesse the benefit of the doubt.

At lunchtime Cynthia was waiting outside the lunchroom door. "You eating with anybody, Kayla?" she asked.

Kayla's eyes lit up. "No. Want to eat with me?"

"Sure," said Cynthia.

They followed the noisy crowd into the cafeteria and found an empty table. "I was beginning to feel like the ugly duckling," said Kayla.

"Really? Well, I think you're pretty."

Kayla laughed softly. "You're kidding. My grandma used to say, 'pretty is only skin deep.' I don't know what she meant, but she was trying to make me feel good."

"You've got pretty green eyes."

Kayla was unbelieving. "You think so?"

Jesse sauntered over to the table balancing a full tray of food with two books tucked under his arm.

"Can I sit with you two?"

"Why not, there's room," Cynthia said.

Jesse looked at Kayla. "You don't mind me sitting here, do you?"

Kayla was surprised that he wanted to sit with two girls. "No, but I do wonder what's wrong with the boys in our class."

"Nothing," he said. "I just want to get to know everybody." The three ate silently for a while before Jesse said, "Kayla, I'll catch a snake for you if you want to observe one for a while. You can let it go whenever you want."

Kayla could tell Jesse was trying to be her friend. She smiled. "Well, okay."

That night Kayla told Johnetta about Jesse's offer. Johnetta looked at her cross-eyed, threw her head back, and gagged. "A snake!" she screeched. "Think about getting your head examined! No snake is coming into *my* room—not while I'm living."

Kayla curled up on her bed and opened the encyclopedia to "Snakes." She was feeling so happy about having two new friends that Johnetta's outburst didn't bother her at all.

CHAPTER ELEVEN

Everybody Goes When the Wagon Comes

The next day, Kayla and Cynthia sat on a bench after school and compared lives.

Cynthia said, "I see you're taking ballet books home to read. You like dancing?"

"You may think I'm silly, but I'm going to be a ballet dancer when I grow up," answered Kayla.

"So am I!" exclaimed Cynthia. "I took lessons for a year before we moved to Chicago."

The two girls grinned at each other. Kayla said, "I want to take lessons more than anything. I called two dance studios, but it's fifteen dollars a lesson. I'm scared to ask Aunt Martha and Uncle Jerome to pay that much."

"Fifteen dollars *is* a lot," said Cynthia. "I heard the park district may be having dance classes. They might be cheaper. Cross your fingers."

Kayla crossed her fingers immediately. As she and Cynthia were leaving the school grounds, a boy bumped into Cynthia, knocking her books to the ground.

"Sorry," he said. He picked up the books.

Kayla recognized him at once. "Say, you were with the boy who took my necklace last summer! What do you want now, *five* dollars?"

He stood up. "Hey, I didn't do nothin'. I can't help what Frank did. He's always in trouble."

"You were with him. You ran when he ran."

"Yeah, but I didn't do nothin'." He looked scared.

"Where's Frank now?" Kayla asked.

"I don't know—he goes to another school."

"When you see him, tell him I want my locket back. It had my mama and daddy's picture in it. My aunt called the police on you two, you know."

He shook his head. "I didn't want him to do it. I don't take people's stuff. My dad would *kill* me."

"Then you oughtn't hang around with people who do."

"Frank's my friend. Anyhow, I didn't know you lived around here." He looked at Kayla apologetically. His light brown eyes matched his sandy-colored braids.

"I do now," said Kayla. "C'mon, Cynthia."

"Look, if I see Frank, I'll tell 'im you want your locket back. I'm really sorry," the boy called.

Kayla didn't answer. "Stupid," she muttered. "Uncle Jerome says, 'Everybody goes when the wagon comes.' "

"What does that mean?" asked Cynthia.

"It means, if you don't want to get blamed for what somebody's doin', don't hang around and watch. Or else when the police wagon comes, they'll get you, too."

"That's good advice. You should have told that to 'Braids.' "

Kayla laughed. "That's a good name for him. He's kinda cute—wonder what class he's in."

"We can find out," said Cynthia. "He *is* cute."

When they got to Kayla's house, Kayla said, "Can you come in and see my practice space?"

"Okay, for just a minute."

They went down to the basement. Aaron was

not around, so Kayla borrowed his radio and found a good station. She showed Cynthia the dance steps she practiced so often, and Cynthia danced for Kayla.

"I never practiced with anyone before," said Kayla. "It's really fun."

"You know all the steps I know," said Cynthia. "You're a really good dancer."

They danced and danced and finally fell on a big overstuffed chair, exhausted. "You need your own tape player with practice tapes," said Cynthia.

"I know, but I don't have enough money yet. Hank is supposed to be looking for me. I saw a used player at a store up the street that I'm going to buy if he doesn't find another one soon."

Cynthia got up. "I gotta go."

"This was cool. Let's do it again," Kayla suggested.

"I'd like to."

The next day after school, Kayla asked Jesse if he knew a boy with sandy-colored braids. "He's probably in seventh grade."

"Yeah, I heard about Ginger. He was always friendly to me even though he was a couple years older. My mom knows his mom and dad. She said they are just about crazy over the shooting."

"What you talking about?" asked Kayla. "I just asked if you know a boy who wears braids."

"That's Ginger," said Jesse. "He was killed last night in a drive-by shooting. He was just standing talking to some other guys. Died right away."

Kayla's books slid out of her arms.

"Oh, my gosh," said Cynthia. "We talked to him yesterday. Didn't we Kayla?"

Kayla nodded. She couldn't speak. She felt as if another piece of her spirit had broken off and drifted away.

Cynthia and Jesse stood talking, but Kayla didn't hear a word they said. Was life always going to be this way—people dying suddenly? She didn't even know Ginger's real name, but she was shocked by this terrible thing. She thought about his family. She thought about her own grief, and she realized how painful it would be for Ginger's family. Maybe it would be worse—he was just a kid.

Jesse handed Kayla her books. He studied her face for a moment. "You all right?"

Kayla nodded as she hugged her books.

"Okay," he said. "I'll see you all tomorrow."

"Bye, Jesse," said Cynthia. "C'mon, Kay."

The girls walked home in silence. At Kayla's gate, Cynthia said, "It's terrible, Kay, but we can't do a thing about it. Try not to be too sad." She put her hand on Kayla's shoulder. "Bye."

At dinner, Kayla told her family about Ginger. "It's not safe to do anything anymore," Aunt Martha said. "There's so much violence in the street! Living in the city is downright scary."

"Without guns, these jokers wouldn't have so much power," said Uncle Jerome angrily. "We can't live our lives in fear. If only we could get guns off the streets!"

"We may never know who did it," said Hank. "It happens every day."

"You're right," said Johnetta. "Who cares if a black kid gets shot down in the street? It wasn't even in the news. I didn't hear a word about it at school."

Hank stood up. "Nobody wants the responsibility of doing something about juvenile crime. The police don't want it, the schools can't handle it, and I guess many parents don't *know* what to do."

"It's hard for me to believe that city officials could

not get a better grip on crime in the streets if they really wanted to," said Uncle Jerome. "We can send men to the moon, but we can't get our kids on course for a better life." He pushed his untouched dessert aside, then left the table.

The next day there was a special school assembly. Kids had only good things to say about Ginger. One student said, "He helped me with math, otherwise I'd have been kicked off the basketball team." Another boy said Ginger had talked him out of cutting school one day and saved him from getting into a lot of trouble.

The principal expressed his sadness that this awful thing had happened to one of his students. He announced a plan to hold meetings for parents, students, and anyone else interested in crime prevention.

Kayla was sorry she'd jumped on Ginger about her necklace. She remembered that he'd objected when Frank took it. Now, of course, she would never get it back. But it didn't matter so much anymore. During history class she wrote a condolence note and on the way out, she dropped it in the box marked "For Ginger's Family."

CHAPTER TWELVE

No Good News

October came, and Jesse still hadn't caught a snake. "They must be hibernating already," he told Kayla during lunch. "We'll probably have an early winter." Kayla didn't really care whether he caught a snake or not. But while she was waiting for Cynthia after school one day, Jesse walked up and handed her a box. "Guess what?" he said, grinning.

Kayla took the box and peeked inside. A garter snake about ten inches long was curled up on a mound of grass. She laughed. "Thanks—you prob'ly caught the last one still hanging around the park."

"Prob'ly." He chuckled. "C'mon, I'll carry it home for you. I need to tell you what to feed it."

"You mean I gotta *feed* it? I thought it would hibernate all winter."

He stopped walking. "C'mon Kayla. It won't hibernate if it's inside where it's warm. Are you planning to let the poor thing go all winter without one or two teeny mice?"

"Give me a break, Jesse. I am *not* going to catch any mice!"

"Okay, a few crunchy cockroaches would do fine."

"Hey, look, maybe you'd better keep it. I'm not into mice and cockroaches."

He burst out laughing. "I'm just kiddin', Kayla. He's okay for now. But if you decide to keep it, we'll talk about food."

She opened the gate to her yard, and he handed her the box. "See you," she said.

Kayla turned the lock on the back door and tiptoed into the hallway. She pushed the box under the hall bench. She stopped and listened before quietly putting her books down. She could hear the sound of voices coming from her bedroom. She was safe.

When Johnetta had company, she didn't pay any attention to Kayla. Sometimes she even asked Kayla to stay out of the room when her girlfriends came by. That was okay with Kayla; Johnetta and her friends talked about nothing but clothes, hair, and boys, boys, boys. Kayla recognized Kramaria's voice.

"But what about Tyree? I thought the two of you were so tight. You said you never wanted to see Heywood again."

"I know, but Tyree wants to get real serious—you know, physical stuff—and I'm not ready for *that,*" said Johnetta. "If I got pregnant, my daddy would kill me *and* Tyree. Besides, Heywood is so dependable—Mom and Dad like him—and I'm tired of not having a boyfriend I can bring home."

Kayla smiled. She crept down the back stairs and turned on the ceiling light. Aaron's animals skittered in their cages. Across the room, her mirror glowed. In the semi-darkness, it appeared bigger and magical, inviting her to step inside. She turned on the radio and borrowed Aaron's old wooden straight-backed chair. It worked better for barre exercises than the folding chair.

Every day she made herself do at least ten minutes of warm-up exercises. Then she danced for fun. She would step inside the mirror on her own make-believe stage, complete with flowers, trees, and a pine-needle path. She danced before an audience, in the glare of brilliant make-believe footlights.

But she never forgot how much she longed to take real ballet lessons. Maybe Aunt Martha could help her figure out a way. It wouldn't hurt to ask—maybe she would do it tonight.

Today Aaron opened the door before she completed her exercises. He checked his cages, fed the animals, then came over to her. "I need my chair, O Great Dancer." Rudely he pulled the chair out from under her hand and dragged it across the floor.

"Turkey," Kayla said under her breath. She put on her shoes and went upstairs.

Johnetta opened the bedroom door. "Hey—there's a letter for you on the hall table."

Kayla's heart almost stopped. She ran to the table. There it was, an envelope with her name neatly printed on the front. She turned it over and read the return address. It wasn't from Daddy or Granpa, but Cheefus! He was the next best person she knew to get a letter from. She opened it carefully and read:

Dear Kayla,

Nothing's the same down here with you gone. I have to admit I miss you a lot. Everybody at school asks me about you. I tell them you like Chicago and will forget about us down on the farm. I like getting letters from you.

Write soon.

Your friend,

Cheefus James Warner

Kayla read it over two times and slipped it into her pocket. Hearing from Cheefus made her happy and sad at the same time. She was glad he liked her letters. She knew that it took a lot of guts for him to write that he missed her. She could see where he had erased it at least once. She went out to the back steps and read the letter again, wondering when she would see him.

She thought about the day of the storm when he had begged her to go fishing, and how funny he had been. She remembered how he had waited at the edge of Gran's garden, how he handed her the little garter snake, how he looked standing in the sun—barefoot, wearing a clean tee-shirt and cut-off jeans that were frayed, not by fashion, but by honest-to-goodness wear. She missed him.

At dinner, Uncle Jerome was not his usual cheerful self. He pushed his food around on his plate and was so quiet that Hank said, "What's up, Dad? Didn't scratch the new car, I hope."

"Nope, nothing like that," said Uncle Jerome, "but I might as well tell you all the bad news. You'll have to know sooner or later." He took a sip of coffee. "I didn't get the promotion I was in line for. Matter of fact, I may have to take a cut in pay, and for some guys it's worse—a half-dozen or more men are out with three weeks' severance pay. Seems like one of our money managers lost a chunk on the stock market."

For a minute nobody said a word. "That means we're in trouble, baby?" Aunt Martha asked at last.

"Naw, not yet, but we better not plan on any trip around the world this year."

There was a long silence.

Aunt Martha got up to get hot coffee. "Nor consider leasing another Town Car in the near future," she murmured.

"I knew it, I *knew* it!" Uncle Jerome yelled. "Damn it, Martha, you always resented my getting the car!"

He jumped up from the table, overturned the chair, and stalked out of the kitchen.

Aunt Martha ran after him. "Aw, Jerome, I was just being funny. I know how bad you wanted that car. We'll make out okay. Where's your sense of humor?" She followed him outside. Kayla heard the car door slam and the sound of the car driving off. Aunt Martha came back inside, shaking her head. She went to her bedroom and closed the door.

Hank righted the chair and headed to his room. Aaron followed him.

Johnetta cradled her face in her hands and breathed hard two or three times. At last she got up and started to clear the table.

Kayla took her plate to the sink. She scraped the food into the garbage pail, rinsed the plate, and put it in the dishwasher. She waited for Johnetta to explain what was going on. Finally she asked, "Did I miss something, Johnetta? Why was Uncle so upset with Aunt Martha?"

"Because she just won an argument they had three months ago. She didn't want him to get that car. But he got it anyway, because he'd been promised the promotion. He even had to dip into their savings, and that's what upset him. Mom may have been teasing but she really was saying 'I told you so.' And let me tell you, nothing makes Daddy madder than hearing that."

"Gran used to say the same thing about Granpa. I remember a story she told one time about him."

Johnetta wiped off the counter and hung up the dishcloths. "Yeah, what was it about?"

"One time she begged him not to buy an ole rooster from Mr. Sager. She told him, 'One rooster is a-plenty.' But he did it anyhow, and guess what happened? That mean ole rooster killed our good rooster, and the hens were scared to come out of the henhouse."

Johnetta laughed. "I bet Granpa was one unhappy soul."

"Sure was. I remember his misery when he found the dead rooster." She giggled. "But he never let on he thought he had done the wrong thing, least not to Gran. I overheard Uncle Walt telling him it was dumb to buy a second rooster; he didn't have enough hens. Granpa admitted Gran had told him the same thing."

Johnetta chuckled. "Don't worry. Mom and

Dad'll get over this. But I don't expect this will be the greatest Christmas ever."

Kayla's needs were few. She had inherited sweaters and other clothes from Johnetta. Her allowance from Granpa took care of school expenses, and the only things she wanted were a tape player, a pair of ballet shoes, and ballet lessons. She was trying to save money—instead of buying lunch at school, she took a sandwich and an apple or cookie from home.

Only Aaron knew how seriously she practiced. She hadn't danced for Aunt Martha and Uncle Jerome yet. Even if they did think she was good enough, how could they afford to pay for lessons now?

Later, sitting in their room, she said to Johnetta, "I'll let you in on a secret."

"What?" Johnetta sat at the dresser examining her face in the mirror.

"You promise not to laugh?"

"Not if it ain't funny."

"It ain't funny to me, but it may be funny to you."

"Try me," said Johnetta, looking at Kayla's serious face.

Kayla picked up Angel. "You know I'm saving for the tape player. I've been practicing in the basement with Aaron's radio. I called two studios about dance classes—I was hoping Auntie and Uncle would let me take lessons." She sat down on the bed, still holding Angel. "Now, I know that won't happen."

Johnetta didn't laugh. She picked up a blusher and thoughtfully dabbed some on her cheeks. "We're not rich, even if Dad had gotten his promotion. Dancing lessons cost more than piano lessons, plus you need all kinds of stuff like shoes and practice outfits." She looked at Kayla. "C'mon, cousin, get a life! Think of something else to wish for."

Kayla looked at her poster of the Harlem Dance Troupe hanging on her wall. Of course Johnetta was right. Who was she to hope for expensive dance lessons?

But Johnetta didn't understand.

Kayla remembered Gran's voice saying, "You dance like an angel, honey girl. You can be a great dancer."

Suddenly Kayla wanted to run away from Chicago, back to South Carolina. She wanted to race with the wind and leap over cotton bushes and low fences. She wanted to feel the warm sand under her bare feet and Balloo's wet tongue licking her face. Sadly, she looked down at Angel, and the rag doll's green embroidered eyes gazed back at her.

Kayla quietly left the bedroom, taking Angel with her. The box with the snake in it was still under the bench in the hall. She picked it up and went out the back door into the yard. She sat on the steps and watched the sinking sun.

What would Gran say to her now—pray for a miracle? Well, maybe it was time to pray again. Gran wanted her to believe in the power of prayer.

Kayla sat on the big rock for a while, thinking about Gran and looking at the faded flowers and browning ground cover. Soon it would be winter. She knelt down, opened the box, and lifted out the wriggling snake. "Go," she whispered. "You're free. Go dance for me!"

She watched the snake disappear in the grass. It occurred to her that Johnetta could be wrong. There might still be a chance. She would write to Granpa. She knew he sent money, but she didn't know how much. She decided to ask Aunt Martha the very next day, when things were calmer.

That night in bed, Kayla stayed awake until Uncle Jerome came home. When she heard him and Aunt Martha talking quietly in the kitchen, she began to drift off. She murmured the prayer Gran had taught her long ago:

Dear God,

For the moments of this day
give me time to stop and pray;
for the love that always hovers near,
for everyone we hold so dear—
thank you.

Somehow she knew that tomorrow would be a better day.

CHAPTER THIRTEEN

Opportunity Knocks

The next two days passed, and Kayla was relieved to see that Aunt Martha and Uncle Jerome were as loving as before. Kayla had not found the right moment to ask Aunt Martha about dancing lessons. Then late one afternoon, just as Kayla had finished practicing, Cynthia knocked on the door.

"Hey Cyn, what's up?" Kayla said, when her friend came in.

"I couldn't wait to tell you! They're going to start dance classes at the park—ballet and tap. Mom says I can sign up."

Kayla closed her eyes. "This may be my miracle. How much will it cost?"

"Forty-five dollars for the fall session, plus you'll need ballet shoes and a leotard."

Kayla said, "I don't have much money saved, but it sounds like a good chance, Cyn. I'll have to ask Aunt Martha. I've been trying to get up nerve to ask her about lessons."

Cynthia grabbed Kayla's hand. "You'll just have to find a way. Forty-five dollars is less than I paid in Detroit. Imagine us taking ballet! Isn't this what you've dreamed about?"

"Yes, but I'll still need . . ." Kayla's voice trailed away. They went outside and sat quietly on the steps.

Finally, Cynthia broke the silence. She looked at Kayla and then at the open shoe box, still on the ground where Kayla had left it two days ago. "What'd you do? Let the snake go?"

"Yeah, it was stupid to take him in the first place. Johnetta woulda had a hissy fit if I took it into the bedroom, and Aaron wouldn't want snakes around his hamsters."

Cynthia said, "What will you tell Jesse?"

"Nothing, except how cute he is."

"Who? Jesse?" Cynthia asked innocently.

"No, silly, the snake."

Both of them laughed at the idea of Kayla telling Jesse he was cute. Cynthia said, "I know what he'd say. 'What you mean I'm cute? Puppies are cute.' "

Kayla said, "I'm pretty sure Jesse doesn't even think about girls liking boys and boys liking girls."

"Jesse is such a nerd—but a nice nerd. I know he likes you," said Cynthia.

"Give me a break!"

Cynthia stood up. "I gotta get home before dark. See you tomorrow."

In the basement, Aunt Martha was taking clothes out of the dryer. Kayla grabbed an armload and set them on the table. She took a deep breath. "Auntie, Cynthia just told me they're starting ballet classes at the park. It costs forty-five dollars. I know this is a really bad time, but do you think Granpa will help me? Dancing is the only thing in the world I want to do."

A worried look spread across Aunt Martha's face. "But you'll need more than forty-five dollars. That's just the beginning."

"I have fifty-three dollars saved," said Kayla. "I can pay the forty-five dollars, and maybe buy ballet shoes and tights later. I'll save every dollar of my allowance. Auntie, I may never get this chance again."

"When do classes begin?"

"Cyn says we have to sign up by Saturday."

Aunt Martha looked at Kayla's pleading eyes.

"Well, I can see you're serious. I didn't realize how important dancing is to you. We'll just have to take a chance that the money will work out. We'll phone Granpa and see what he says."

Kayla was so happy she could hardly keep from dancing. She decided to wait until after dinner to tell Johnetta her news and was surprised when Johnetta said, "Well, you're certainly persistent. Maybe you *do* have what it takes to be a ballerina. I see you gazing at Stephanie Dabney's picture all the time."

"Why not?" said Kayla. "Stephanie's my idol." She looked at her poster of the Harlem Dance Troupe. "If Stephanie can do it, so can I."

She put on her pajamas and did a couple of graceful turns, finishing with a grand bow.

"Um, very nice," murmured Johnetta. She turned off her light. "Good luck, cousin, good luck."

"Thanks, Johnetta." Kayla climbed into bed. In the darkness she whispered, "Thanks, Gran—the prayer worked."

Saturday, Kayla and Cynthia walked to the park. It was a breezy October morning, and the sun was warm and bright. "Gosh, I bet Daddy will be glad to know I have this chance," said Kayla. "Think he'll ever know?"

"Sure, why not?" answered Cynthia. "You'll grow up and become famous; then you can find him and tell him yourself."

"But I want him to know *now*, so he can help me become famous."

"But he's not here, and you've got a nice big family to help you. I never worry about my dad. When I see him, fine. If I don't, that's okay, too. My brother still misses him a lot."

"You're smarter than I am," said Kayla. "I'll never stop missing my dad, and I don't even remember what he looks like."

Ms. Pacini, the dance teacher, was a petite, dark-haired woman with huge brown eyes. She greeted Cynthia and Kayla warmly and said to Kayla, "Gracious, you're already as tall as I am. Such nice long legs. Come, let's see if you're going to be a great dancer." Kayla blushed and looked at the other girls. She towered over each of them by almost a head. At school, there were other girls as tall as she. But here she felt like a gawky, ungraceful giant.

Ms. Pacini clapped her hands, "All right, class, we

will play the music. You will dance. Do anything that comes to mind. Pretend you are dancing alone or for your family. I want to see what you can do." She started the music and all the girls, except Kayla, waltzed around to *Swan Lake*. Kayla stood still. She couldn't think of a single step. She couldn't lift her arms or move her body.

Cynthia waltzed over and touched Kayla's shoulder. "C'mon, *dance*, Kayla!" she urged.

Kayla remained motionless—a tree without a bending wind.

The music stopped before she recovered. "That was very nice," Ms. Pacini said. "We will begin our exercise routines at the barre." She looked at Kayla with an understanding smile. "Stage fright is a natural feeling for dancers or any artists. You'll learn to work with it."

Kayla relaxed a bit. At the barre, she was able to do each exercise as Ms. Pacini directed. She needed some position coaching, but the teacher complimented her posture and flexibility.

After class, Ms. Pacini announced that although dance slippers retailed for $19.00, she could get them for a discounted price of $14.75. She would measure their feet and order shoes for those who wanted them.

If Granpa doesn't help, I'll have to go without milk and extra stuff for a month before I have enough money for shoes and a tape player, too, Kayla thought. She caught Cynthia's eye, and Cynthia smiled reassuringly. Kayla smiled back. She knew Cynthia had guessed what she was thinking—good friends could do that.

That night after they had finished their spaghetti, Aunt Martha announced that Uncle Jerome had lost two of his major accounts. "That's another blow since he already had to take a cut in salary."

Hank cleared his throat, and Johnetta put down her fork. Aaron said, "Are we going to be poor?"

Aunt Martha reached over and patted his head. "I plan to get a job before that happens. It may not be easy for me to get a good job—I haven't worked in fifteen years. I can type, but I know very little about computers. I may have to go back to school."

"I'll get a part-time job," offered Hank.

"Not yet," said Aunt Martha. "School is more important, and I'll need you to help at home."

Kayla caught her breath. She said softly, "What

about my ballet lessons? Is that going to be too much?"

Aunt Martha looked at Kayla. "We'll manage that. It's not a lot, and it's an opportunity that doesn't happen often." She got up from the table. "Please, all of you, look happy when Dad comes in later. He's miserable enough for everyone. We'll be all right."

Two days later, Aunt Martha told the children that she was going to do office work temporarily, in a nearby taffy-apple factory. "Each of you will have to take on more responsibility. I'll put a job list on the refrigerator. Sign up for the job and time you want. You may negotiate with one another."

"Can I cook?" asked Aaron.

"And kill us all?" said Johnetta. "Get real! You can take out the garbage."

Aaron persisted. "I can make an egg sandwich like Mama used to make. You take a slice of bread and cut out a circle with a juice glass. Put the bread in a pan with butter. Then beat the egg and pour it in the circle and cook it. Is that right, Mama?"

"That's right, honey, and you can cook that for me anytime."

Hank said, "I can make my famous chili one night a week."

"Sure—you may find your real talent is cooking rather than baseball," said Johnetta.

"Not likely," grumbled Hank.

Kayla talked Aaron into selling his hamsters. With Uncle Jerome's and Aunt Martha's permission, they hung a sign on the corner fence which read, BABY HAMSTERS FOR SALE—$1.00 EACH. They sold six in three days, and Aaron split the money with Kayla. Against his will, she hugged him. "Four dollars more, and I can buy ballet slippers!"

"Yep, just remember next time we need hamster food, you get to pay for half of it."

After ballet class on Saturday, Aunt Martha said, "You got a priority letter from Granpa, Kayla. It's on the kitchen table."

Carefully, Kayla opened the letter. Inside was a check for two hundred dollars! Granpa had sold the calf. He wrote, "Ancy was not too happy, but this seemed like the big moment for you. Go on and dance, honey girl."

"Wow, wow, wow!" sang Kayla as she hugged

Aunt Martha. "Now I can take lessons the whole year."

That very same day Hank went with Kayla to buy a tape player he had found. He took a rap tape along and tested the machine in the store at full volume. When he was done, he told Kayla the player had a good sound for its size and price. Kayla knew then that if she ever had to choose a big brother, Hank would be the one.

When Kayla told Ms. Pacini about the tape player, she said, "Wonderful! Let's choose a practice tape for you, Kayla."

Kayla practiced diligently—even on weekends. The most fun times were when Cynthia came by after school and they practiced together. Kayla wished her daddy knew about her dance lessons. She felt sure that somehow Gran knew what was happening—maybe even that she was responsible for Kayla's good fortune.

CHAPTER FOURTEEN

The Audition

Two weeks after Kayla got her ballet shoes, Ms. Pacini announced that a local theater company would be auditioning children to dance in its Christmas performance of the *Nutcracker*. "I hope some of you will audition," she told the class.

"There isn't much time but since we've been working with the music, you're familiar with it. For the tryout, you can use the dance routine we've been practicing. You'll have to be what we call 'a quick study,' that is, practice hard and learn fast. Who's interested?" Several hands went up.

"Why not you, Kayla?" asked Ms. Pacini. "You know the routine well."

"I'm not sure I'm good enough—plus I don't know how I would get to the audition."

"I'll drive you," said Ms. Pacini. "You'll never know if you're good enough until you try. It will be a valuable experience. The auditions will take place the first Saturday in November. Girls, take a permission slip home and have one of your parents sign it. Bring it back by Wednesday."

Kayla, Cynthia, Claudette, and Nina decided to audition. Ms. Pacini made them work extra hard. The other three girls complained, but Kayla didn't. She liked to push herself.

One evening Johnetta stopped by the park and watched the four practice. She said to Kayla, "You guys are pretty good."

Cynthia said, "Gosh, you're lucky. I'd give anything to have a big sister as smart and pretty as Johnetta."

"I know," admitted Kayla. "I'm lucky in a lot of ways. Lucky you're my friend. I don't know what I'd do without you."

"Me, too," said Cynthia.

Kayla practiced every moment she could. The whole family was excited about the audition. Kayla and Aaron were cleaning up after dinner one night, when Aaron said suddenly, "I knew you'd be famous one day. Why do you think I put up with you dancing all the time?"

Kayla giggled. "This doesn't mean I'm going to be famous. Granpa used to say, 'Don't count your chickens before they hatch.' "

"Well, you better be famous, else I'll have to take back all the braggin' I did to my friends."

"I think you'd better not brag unless I pass the audition."

"Too late—I already bragged."

She looked at him for a second or so, then reached out and touched his shoulder. "Thanks, Aaron. That may be all the luck I need."

The night before the audition, Johnetta looked up from a romance novel she was reading and said to Kayla, "You can wear my new white body suit over your purple tights. I've been saving it for something special." Kayla's much-washed purple leotard was hanging on the door. "Yours is a mess."

"Wow! Thanks, Johnetta. I'll take good care of it and try not to sweat."

Johnetta laughed. "Well, I'm not counting on that!"

The morning came too quickly for Kayla. "If only

I had another month to practice," she said as she got dressed.

Johnetta accentuated Kayla's eyes with a little green eye shadow and French-braided her hair with white ribbon intertwined. "You look quite classic, cousin. Like a ballerina should."

Aunt Martha came into the room. "Here—since your ears aren't pierced, wear these little pearl ear bobs. Don't worry 'bout losing them. They're not expensive, but they are pretty."

"Oh, thanks, Aunt Martha!" said Kayla, her eyes shining with happy tears. "Goodness, I feel like a fairy princess."

"You look like one," said Uncle Jerome, sticking his head into the bedroom. "We know you'll dance like one."

The doorbell rang.

"That's Cyn," said Kayla. "We have to meet Ms. Pacini at the park." She pulled her jeans on over her tights and picked up her ballet slippers. She gave her aunt and uncle and Johnetta a hug, and ran down the hall. Aaron and Hank were standing at the front door. She hugged them, too. As she and Cynthia left, Hank called, "Good luck you two! Break a leg, Kay!"

Kayla and Cynthia zipped their jackets against the cold November wind and hurried up the street. Cynthia said, "You look super with eye makeup."

"So do you," replied Kayla. Cynthia was wearing a purple leotard and white tights. Her long blond hair was also braided, and her mother had tied it up with black ribbons.

"Your family is great, you know. They like you a lot," said Cynthia.

Kayla realized quite suddenly that she felt really close to her family. It was a good feeling. She said, "I know. We fight and fuss, but we make up. Guess big families are like that."

Cynthia said softly, "I guess."

Ms. Pacini was waiting at the park. All the girls piled into her mini-van. As they fastened their seat belts, she said, "The competition will be tough, but even if you don't win, it will be a good experience. You'll get a taste of what it's like to be professional. I've danced in fifteen ballet performances. I'm sure I have auditioned for fifty. Each time it gets easier."

The more Ms. Pacini talked, the more frightened Kayla became. She counted what she thought of as her handicaps. First, she didn't have her locket. Next, she was taller than most kids her age. She'd had real dance lessons for only a little while.

Then, too, she had watched many ballets on television, but she had never seen a black ballerina dance in a classical ballet. She had heard Gran and other people talk about racial prejudice all of her life. She heard about people being mistreated because of their color, but except for the man's awful remark that day in the pet store, such a thing had never happened to her. Would it happen now? Gran's voice came from somewhere deep inside her memory. "You can do anything you set your heart on, honey girl."

Remembering her grandmother's words encouraged her. She tried not to think about the handicaps. She tried to imagine how it would feel to dance in a real ballet.

At the theater, Ms. Pacini jumped out of the van. "Remember now, relax and follow the music. If you forget the routine, make one up and keep going till you find your place."

The theater was noisy and confusing, with kids everywhere. They were not allowed to go backstage, so Ms. Pacini led her students to a corner where they shed their outer clothes and put on their ballet slippers. A girl came and gave Ms. Pacini a package of numbers along with instructions. Ms. Pacini pinned a set of numbers on each girl. Kayla was number twenty-one. Cynthia was twenty-eight; Nina, twenty-nine; and Claudette, number thirty-five.

Promptly at 10:00, a man spoke into the microphone. "Please be quiet; it will make our job much easier. You'll be called in groups of twenty. Start dancing when the director gives the signal, and perform the routines you learned for this audition. When the music stops, please leave the stage. Your teachers will be sent the numbers of the winners when we finish tallying. Thank you for coming, and good luck to all of you."

He walked away, and another man came to the podium. "Will those wearing numbers one through twenty come on stage?" Dancers from all over the theater scrambled to the stage. The music started, and the audition began.

Kayla and Cynthia squeezed each other's hands. Kayla was glad their group had not been called first. She watched intently as the first group danced.

"They're really good," said Kayla.

"Not as good as we are," said Claudette. "Especially you, Kayla."

Kayla smiled nervously. She had memorized every note of the music. She hoped that would make it easier to concentrate on the steps.

The music ended, and she heard the stage manager say, "Thank you for coming. Please leave the theater as quietly as you can." He waited until the stage was cleared and people stopped talking. Kayla thought her heart would beat clear out of her chest. She whispered to Cynthia, "Lordy, Cyn, I'm scared to death. I can't move."

The stage manager called out, "Numbers twenty-one through forty, please come on stage."

Kayla's group headed for the stage. Her knees felt rubbery and weak. She said to herself, "I can do this. I know I can." She felt Cynthia's hand on her arm.

Kayla barely had time to look out at the huge theater before the director said, "Space yourselves, please," but that look was long enough for her to know that the stage was where she was born to be. The music began. She breathed deeply and thought only of her dance steps. She caught the feeling and dissolved into the music. It was magic; she was there with the Nutcracker, the tin soldiers, and the Sugar Plum Fairy.

In too short a time, the audition was over. The director said, "Thank you. Please leave quietly. You will hear from us." He did not look at Kayla when she passed by.

CHAPTER FIFTEEN

The Wonder of It All

On Sunday and Monday, Kayla and Cynthia called each other every hour. On Tuesday, they went by the park. Ms. Pacini told Cynthia she had been accepted. So had Claudette and Nina. "Kayla's results didn't come today—perhaps tomorrow."

Kayla's heart skipped a beat, and she felt a little sick. Suppose she wasn't chosen? "I'll just die," she thought.

"Now, be patient, Kayla; we know you made it. You were one of the best dancers," assured Ms. Pacini. "Don't worry."

Kayla smiled weakly, but she could think of nothing to say. On the way home, Cynthia tried to cheer her up. "Sure you made the cut; you're better than all of us. Maybe they're gonna make you the star." Kayla was still anxious.

It was the longest night of Kayla's life. Aunt Martha and Johnetta tried to console her. "At least wait a few days," said Johnetta. "You said yourself that hundreds of kids tried out. Maybe there was a mix-up."

Sure enough, the next day Ms. Pacini's eyes sparkled with excitement as she met Kayla at the door. "You made it, Kayla. They called this morning. I don't know why your name didn't come with the others, but it doesn't matter. You're in!"

Kayla stood shivering with happiness. "Gosh, Ms. Pacini, I never felt so strong and so wiggly at the same time in my life! I was scared to death!"

"I know, Kayla, but I wasn't worried at all. You're a natural dancer, with such delightful presence. I have difficulty believing you've never had lessons before."

Kayla blushed. "Thanks, Ms. Pacini," she whispered. "I love to dance more than anything. My daddy is a dancer, and so was my mother."

"So talent runs in the family. That's an advantage!

Well, rehearsals will be Wednesdays after school and Saturday mornings."

As Kayla and Cynthia left the building a boy stepped in front of them. Kayla recognized him right away. It was the boy who had taken her locket—the boy Ginger had called Frank.

He said, "I got something that belongs to you. Gingerboy asked me for it the night he was killed. Him getting killed was a real bummer. He was no gang member—he was my best friend." He handed her the locket and walked away, but not before his eyes filled with tears.

Kayla just stood. Finally, she yelled, "Hey, wait!" She and Cynthia caught up with Frank. "We hate it about Ginger, too," Kayla said. "He told me you were his friend. Everybody said what a neat kid he was, huh, Cyn?"

"That's right," said Cynthia. "It was an awful thing to happen, losing your best friend like that."

"Well, yeah, thanks," said Frank. "Sometimes I feel like it was my fault. He had just left me when it happened. Maybe if I'd been with him . . . well, at least you got your necklace back."

Kayla said, "This locket was always my lucky

charm. I thought I lost my chance to dance in the ballet because you took it, but my chance came anyway."

Frank looked at her for a moment. "I don't know about lucky charms. I do what I can and hope for the best."

"I bet you do. Well, thanks for bringing back my necklace."

"Yeah, I was wrong taking it." He stood looking at Kayla. "You dancing in a ballet, huh? Wow, that's something. Good luck."

"Thanks—if you want to come, there may be some extra tickets," said Kayla.

"You kidding? Me go to a ballet? The guys would put me down for sure." He walked away.

Kayla held her locket tightly in the palm of her hand. It was warm and comforting, but she knew that she'd give it up if it would bring Ginger back.

"You know what, Cynthia, I still believe in lucky charms—guardian angels, too."

Cynthia laughed and said, "Whatever works. C'mon, Kay, it's getting dark. We may *need* a guardian angel if we don't get home." They ran all the way.

Thanksgiving was upon them before Kayla had gotten through the Halloween candy Aaron had given her. For the first time in her life she hadn't gone trick-or-treating. She felt too old to get into the spirit of the day. Instead of going out, she practiced.

Two days before Thanksgiving, Kayla and Johnetta went grocery shopping. Aunt Martha had given them a list. She said to buy a big turkey; they cost less per pound.

Aunt Martha cooked the turkey with cornbread stuffing, and she made peach cobbler. Johnetta made the salad and prepared the collard greens. Kayla peeled the sweet potatoes that she had washed and microwaved the day before. She cut them up and added melted butter, brown sugar, and spices. The boys shucked fresh corn that Uncle Jerome had found in a Mexican produce market. Then they set the table.

When the family sat down to dinner, each person had to say what he or she was especially thankful for. Kayla said, "I'm thankful for my family, school, and the chance to study ballet."

Dinner was delicious. Kayla ate quietly. She was

thinking about her daddy. At last she said, "I wrote Daddy about the ballet. I don't understand why he just forgot me."

"He didn't, honey. I don't understand it, either, but I know he is the one missing the most," Aunt Martha said.

The first week of December was crammed with shopping, writing cards, and practicing. Suddenly there was only one week left before the performances began. Kayla, Cynthia, Claudette, and Nina would be dancing in the first act, where the children were at a Christmas Eve party. Every night Kayla dreamed she was dancing a different part in the ballet.

Finally it was opening night. Johnetta rode along with the group to help Ms. Pacini with details and makeup. Aunt Martha said Uncle Jerome had an errand, but he'd be there before curtain time. She, Hank, and Aaron had driven with Cynthia's mother and brother. Hank had never seen a ballet and was curious. Aaron complained, "My friends will think I'm flaky, going to a ballet." Aunt Martha told him he was going, and that was that. Kayla knew he wouldn't have missed it for anything.

While Kayla and the others were waiting for the curtain to go up, Kayla got a glimpse of the huge auditorium, filled with hundreds of people sitting in levels that seemed to vanish into the ceiling. Their own families, dressed in their Sunday best, were seated third row center.

Johnetta came into the room where the dancers were waiting and sat down next to Kayla. She whispered, "Girl, have I got a surprise for you!"

"What?" asked Kayla.

"If I told you, it wouldn't be a surprise, silly. You'll be happy—don't worry."

"Is it a present?"

"Sort of," answered Johnetta. "You'll find out soon's the show is over, not a minute before." She fussed with Kayla's red braided rag-doll wig and added a little more blusher to her cheeks. Kayla wore a green-and-white checked dress with ruffles on the sleeves and skirt. Long green stockings with black ballet slippers completed her costume. The other girls' costumes were the same as Kayla's but different colors.

"Flowers," whispered Kayla. "I bet it's flowers."

"Could be, but I'm not telling," Johnetta teased.

Kayla looked around at the other dancers in their wonderful costumes. She saw the Sugar Plum Fairy, Marie, and the Nutcracker. Toy soldiers with high top hats and cardboard guns paraded through the hall. The owl and the big fat rat looked pretty scary.

Ms. Pacini came over and said, "The costumes are great; you all look like real dolls, thanks to Johnetta's makeup skills. Better warm up a bit, it won't be long now."

At last the backstage director came in and said, "Five minutes. Places!" The dancers scampered to their places and waited for cues.

As Kayla's group entered side stage, she noticed an African-American man standing in the wings holding a bouquet of yellow roses. Could it be...? The curtain rose. There was no time to look more closely.

The conductor came on stage, and the applause exploded in Kayla's ears. The overture began. Kayla listened as the music skipped through the main themes. Her hands felt sticky, and sweat beaded her upper lip. Finally the director whispered, "Okay, let's go!"

She ran to her spot, and the dance began.

Kayla's group pirouetted over to the huge Christmas tree and curtsied to Marie. Looking into the audience, Kayla imagined all eyes were on her. She felt weak and scared, but she followed the music, remembering all the steps. She thought of her magic mirror and told herself, "I can do this. I *can* dance!" And in a few moments she forgot the audience and blended with the music. Her heart was like a drum beating the rhythm with the toy soldiers. She waltzed and pirouetted with the other dancers around the massive Christmas tree. It *was* magic!

As the curtain fell, Kayla heard the deafening applause. Claudette, Cynthia, Nina, and Kayla ran off stage and hugged each other again and again.

"One time I thought I'd die when I looked out at the audience and saw everybody looking at me," said Kayla.

"That would have been better than throwing up," said Claudette. "I felt sick. There were so many people!"

"We didn't," said Cynthia. "We didn't die or throw up. We didn't even forget our dance."

"Did you notice the group of boys who got mixed up?" asked Nina.

"I bet their teacher is mad," whispered Claudette.

Her part over, Kayla could relax and enjoy the rest of the performance. The first two rows of the theater had been reserved for the student dancers and their teachers. They were ushered from backstage during the first intermission.

Kayla had never been to a real performance before. She'd only seen bits and pieces of this one at rehearsals, and most of the bumpy dress rehearsal. Tonight everything flowed. She liked the "Dance of the Sugar Plum Fairy" best. She knew some of the steps to the "Waltz of the Flowers" because Ms. Pacini had taught them to the class. She had never seen the "Russian Dance" before; it was very athletic and exciting.

After the final curtain call, Kayla and the others waited backstage for their families. Johnetta came into the room followed by the man carrying yellow roses. The man stopped and looked at Kayla. He smiled. Kayla's heart stopped.

A girl ran across the room from behind Kayla into his outstretched arms. "Nicole," he said softly. "My own little ballerina. You were wonderful."

"C'mon girl," said Johnetta as she grabbed Kayla's

hand. "They're waiting for us."

"Lordy, for a minute I thought it was Daddy." Kayla laughed nervously.

"You serious? Gosh, that's a bummer."

"He stared at me, too, and even smiled."

"Maybe you look like somebody in his family."

Johnetta put her hand on Kayla's shoulder. "I know not being in touch with your dad is bad news, but it could be worse. You still have a whole family." She hugged Kayla lightly. "You okay?"

Kayla looked at Johnetta's concerned face. "I *am* okay," she said. "Let's go."

"Look!" cried Johnetta, as she pointed to a group headed in their direction.

Uncle Jerome and a boy who was taller than Aaron were walking toward them, and yes, Granpa! She knew it was Granpa! And then she recognized the boy. Cheefus! What was Cheefus doing here?

She ran into Granpa's outstretched arms. He hugged her for a long time before holding her at arm's length and looking at her face. "My, my, you're growin' up fast, honey girl." His eyes were shining with unshed tears.

Cheefus stood waiting patiently. At last Kayla

turned from Granpa. "Cheefus! Wow, this is a big surprise!" He hugged her and handed her three pink roses. "My favorite, how did you know?" Huge happy tears rolled down Kayla's face as Cheefus kissed her on the cheek.

He whispered, "Since everybody at school couldn't come, they pitched in and helped me buy a ticket. We don't want you to forget us. You're famous back home. Story in both newspapers. I brought them for your scrapbook."

"I can't forget you all, especially Ms. Pickens. She gave me my poster and picture to dream on. My first dream came true tonight."

"I can see now it's been worth all the trouble," said Johnetta, looking at Kayla's joyful face.

The rest of the family had stood aside and watched this special reunion. Now Aunt Martha, Uncle Jerome, Hank, and Aaron took turns hugging Kayla. Hank handed her a bouquet of flowers. "From all of us—to our star."

"Not from me," said Aaron. "My present is waiting for you at home."

"Really?" asked Kayla. "What is it?"

"It was going to be a surprise but you might as

well know. I'm giving you that straight-back chair you always use when I'm not there. Now you can use it when I'm *there.*"

Kayla almost started to cry again, but she knew better than to cry in front of Aaron. She did hug him again—to his dismay—and said, "I love you, Aaron."

Kayla held Cheefus's hand. He had come to see her dance. Granpa and the rest of her family—Aunt Martha, Uncle Jerome, Hank, Johnetta, and Aaron—were all there. Her best friend, Cynthia, stood nearby.

And for one long second, through the noise of the theater, Kayla could clearly hear Gran's voice. "You danced like an angel, honey girl, just like angel!"

ABOUT THE AUTHOR

Darwin McBeth Walton was born and grew up in Charlotte, North Carolina. She spent many happy summers on her grandparents' farm in South Carolina.

She studied music and ballet at Johnson C. Smith University, Howard University, and the Chicago Conservatory of Music, and enjoyed a brief stage career. After her children were born, she decided to teach. She taught in Elmhurst, Illinois, public schools for twenty years and is currently a member of National-Louis University's adjunct faculty. In 1997, she was selected as one of ten outstanding women leaders of DuPage County, Illinois.

Walton has written for numerous educational publications and is the author of *What Color Are You?* and *Ebony in the Classroom.* She lives with her husband in Lombard, Illinois.